THE PURSUED PATRIOT

Georgia Patriots Romance

CAMI CHECKETTS

Birch River
PUBLISHING

FREE BOOK

Sign up for Cami's newsletter and receive a free ebook copy of *The Resilient One: A Billionaire Bride Pact Romance* here.

CHAPTER ONE

Mike Kohler walked onto the wooden plank patio of the outdoor restaurant on the picturesque Hilton Head Island, searching for a seat. He hated eating alone but supposed he'd have to get used to it. At least now the Patriots were back in season, and most meals would be eaten with the team, or he could get a teammate or friend in Atlanta to go out with him.

Dating any of the beautiful women who pursued him wasn't a risk he was willing to take. After most dates, he'd get crazy emails from his stalker, claiming she was going to dismember his date, or worse, especially if he dared to go out with the same woman twice. The threats had escalated lately, and some of the women had sent him texts about weird accidents happening to them. Accidents that were exactly like the threat issued. Quite often, he'd get a follow-up email explaining how the accident could've been fatal if this had been a second date. Luckily none of them had been seriously injured, but it was so creepy that he hardly dared go out with a woman even once. He refused to involve anyone else in the psychotic web of his stalker.

He was here on Hilton Head Island, off the coast of South Carolina, because he'd been ordered by the Patriots' owner, Bucky Buchanan, to "get out of Dodge and clear your head of that idiot stalker for a weekend." As this was their bye weekend, he'd been excused from practice. Missing practice made him feel out of sorts, but at least he now had the best security money could buy. Sutton Smith had recently assigned Gunner and Lily Steele to protect him. He liked the newlywed couple, a lot. Gunner was a tougher-than-nails ex-Navy SEAL and Mike's teammate Preston Steele's brother. The connection was nice and made him more comfortable than the bodyguards Bucky had been providing the past few years. Lily had an interesting past with her mother being Bella Jolie, a famous actress who had cracked and tried to kill Gunner and Lily for publicity. Mike might have a crazy stalker, but at least he had a nice, normal family.

Gunner and Lily had a connecting suite to his at the Hilton. Mike knew with them close by, no stalker would hurt him, but he was more concerned about her hurting a woman he might find interesting. For the present time, his dating life had screeched to a halt.

Gunner and Lily walked into the restaurant on his four o'clock and took an intimate table a few over from where he sat. He glanced around the beach-front restaurant, loving the view and the scent of salty air mingled with grilling meat. He was looking over the menu when a friendly voice greeted him, "Welcome to the Crabby Grill." A redheaded girl, who looked barely out of braces, set an ice water down in front of him and grinned. "You want something different to drink? A recommendation for dinner?"

"Thanks." Mike took a swallow of the water and peered at the menu. "I'd love a strawberry daiquiri, virgin, and yeah, what are your recommendations?"

She wrinkled her nose, and her blue eyes sparkled. "Well, first, I'm going to recommend that you take my friend, Shar, out on a date. She's a huge fan of yours. I mean, crazy huge!"

"Excuse me?" Mike straightened. So he'd been recognized. It was fine, it happened, but hopefully it wouldn't bring his stalker here. If this child wanted him to take her teenage friend out, they were both in for a disappointment.

The redhead tilted her head toward the open doors that led to the kitchen. Mike followed her gaze, ready to explain that he didn't date teenagers. There was another teenager there, a pixy blonde, but she tugged someone else to the opening, and his eyes caught on an absolutely exquisite woman. She was maybe in her mid-twenties, close to his own age. She had olive skin, long, dark hair, and deep brown eyes. Wearing a flowered apron over a tank top and shorts, she was obviously fit and lean. Her gaze met his, and his stomach swooped. She wanted to meet him? If only he felt safe dating. He'd take her out in a second.

There was something so familiar about her, and suddenly it struck him. *Her friend, Shar?* No, that woman was ... Ally Steele, his friend Preston's wife, and he definitely shouldn't be checking her out. He remembered Ally being more rounded, not quite as lean, but he really shouldn't be analyzing her shape at all.

He whipped back around, and the redhead was watching him expectantly. "So?" She winked. "Shar? What'd you think? She's pretty, huh?"

He thought this girl was completely unprofessional. "About those recommendations?" he asked.

Her mouth drooped, and her blue eyes filled with confusion. "You didn't think she was pretty? What are you, blind?"

Mike clenched the menu. "She is gorgeous, but that woman is Ally Steele, my friend's wife."

The redhead's grin returned. "No! Shar is Ally's twin sister, and this is her restaurant. You think she's gorgeous. Yes!" She pumped a fist in the air.

Mike's shoulders relaxed as understanding filled him, but then he went back to thinking about how unprofessional this was. Shar Heathrow, Ally's sister, owned this restaurant. He remembered now from Preston and Ally's wedding that Ally had a twin, but he'd never met her, just admired her from afar. Why was she hiring teenagers to be waitresses and fix her up on dates? Did they not have child labor laws in South Carolina?

"You stay right here. I'll go get your daiquiri and tell Shar she *has* to come meet you. Oh, and I'll get you some fried pickles, on the house. They're delicious. And a big guy like you? Get the platter—crab, lobster, steak, and barbecued chicken. You'll love it." She squealed happily and took off toward the kitchen entrance.

Mike's head was whirling as she skipped away from him. He'd love to meet Shar officially, but it might be awkward after the young girl tried to set them up. He couldn't imagine Shar instigating that, but he didn't know anything about her.

He waited and waited, shifting impatiently in the chair. He tried to focus on the calming beach waves and the delicious scents emanating from the kitchen, but knowing Shar Heathrow was coming to talk to him had him sitting straighter and trying to appear confident yet relaxed. He didn't dare take his phone out and check his emails, so he didn't look so desperate, but he was more worried about looking like one of those guys who couldn't disconnect. As time ticked by, it was getting a little unnerving wondering when she'd appear. He didn't think it was smart to date, but his stalker couldn't be watching him right now. Nobody knew they'd left Atlanta except Bucky, Gunner, Lily, and Sutton Smith, their boss. There was nothing wrong with simply meeting a beautiful woman.

He kept sneaking glances back at the kitchen, and suddenly, Lily was slowly walking by him, her blue eyes full of concern.

"Everything okay?" she whispered when she reached him, pulling her long, blonde hair forward to cover her face.

"Yeah."

She nodded and walked on past. Had he looked that nervous? He would've done the signal if he was in distress, but he must be really fidgety for Lily to approach him.

Someone rushed out of the kitchen entrance, and he straightened his back and turned slightly with a welcoming smile. His smile drooped a little bit when the redhead came back out alone. She set the daiquiri down and a plate of fried pickles. She looked ... upset.

"Thanks," Mike said.

"I'm sorry," she burst out in almost a wail then she wrapped her arms tightly around herself and rocked back and forth.

"It's okay." Mike tried for a soothing tone. He knew he was big and often intimidated people at six-six and two-fifty, but this girl didn't seem afraid of him. She was more frustrated and in despair. "Are you okay?"

"Yes!" She flung her hands around. "Shar's too nice to ever get mad at me, but I think I embarrassed her. When I told her what I'd said, and what you'd said, her face got all stiff, and she said she was too busy cooking to come meet you right now, and then she rushed off out back, hiding in the alley behind the restaurant. I'm no dummy, okay? I can read between the lines. I messed it up, and now she's never going to meet you, and you're like her hero. I mean she even has posters of you all over the kitchen. I wouldn't be surprised if she has some at her house. *That's* how much she loves you, and now I've messed up your cute-meet. Oh, crap-shooters!"

The girl finally stopped her rant, and Mike should've been worried that half the restaurant was staring at him, but something was churning in his gut. Posters of him? Her hero? How much she loved him? It was an absolutely crazy thought ... but at the same time, it wasn't. Could Shar Heathrow be his stalker? He glanced pointedly at Gunner and Lily, rubbed at his jaw, and then rubbed his hand over his hair. Lily's eyes widened, and Gunner looked more serious than usual, which was saying something as he was a pretty stiff guy, except for with his wife.

Mike stood, towering over the teenage redhead. "You didn't

mess it up," he tried to say reassuringly. "I'll go find Shar, talk it out with her. You said she went behind the restaurant?"

The girl's eyes filled with relief. "Yeah." She pointed. "Thanks."

Mike threw a couple of twenties down on the table, and she raised a questioning eyebrow. "Just in case I don't make it back." He forced a smile, but his gut was churning. If Shar was his stalker, he wouldn't dare eat anything she cooked. He was going to try to play charming and maybe get the truth out of her. If only Gunner and Lily agreed.

He eased to the side of the restaurant, waiting in the shadows. Gunner and Lily approached him and moved in close. "What's going on?" Gunner asked.

"This is Shar Heathrow's restaurant."

"Ally's sister? Like my sister-in-law's sister, so we're basically related?" Lily said in her usual funny way of phrasing things. "That's a cool coincidence."

"I don't know what to think. The little redhead wanted me to meet her, said I'm her hero and she has posters of me at the restaurant and possibly even at her home." He arched an eyebrow. "Then she was all upset because she said Shar got embarrassed and took off behind the restaurant."

"Posters of you?" Lily repeated. "A grown woman? That's ... a bit sketchy."

"She could easily be the stalker," Gunner got there quick, his dark eyes full of concern.

"That's what I wondered. She'd have access to a lot of information about me through Preston and Ally."

"Didn't you meet her at their wedding?" Lily asked.

"No. I saw her and thought she was beautiful, but it was a big wedding, and I never got close enough to talk to her."

"Hmm." Gunner was rubbing at his short beard. "We can check into her. Let's go find food somewhere else, though. I don't want to eat anything your stalker might have cooked."

Mike nodded, but he had another idea. "What if I approach her with you two following me? I could gain her trust and see if she reveals anything." It made him a little nervous, but if there was any chance to catch this stalker and move on with his life, he'd take it.

"That could be dangerous," Lily said.

"You two can keep me in your sights. It's not like my stalker has ever threatened me, only the women I date."

They both still looked dubious.

"Come on. I'm sick of living like this." Not being able to date sucked, but he also hated being commanded to miss practice. Football had been his life for so long that he felt off not being with his team and working hard for the next goal. "'We can check into her' might take months to come up with another dead-end."

They'd been checking into his college girlfriend, Meredith, who had been royally ticked when Mike dumped her days after signing on with the Patriots his senior year. She'd claimed he'd dumped her because he wanted to go date famous women, didn't want to share his money and thought she'd hurt his obsession with football. He'd actually dumped her because she was too possessive and freaked out if he gave too much time to football, or if another woman so much as smiled at him. Sutton's men hadn't found anything on her though, besides the fact she'd moved to his hometown of Birmingham after she got her master's degree, went to his dad's church, and was close friends with his sister. None of those things made her a stalker, just made it awkward trying to avoid her when he went home.

Lily's blue eyes were wary, but Gunner nodded. "If you want to try it. Maybe talk her into a walk on the beach. Stay in open areas at all times. We'll be close."

Mike clapped him on the shoulder. "Thanks, man." He headed for the back of the restaurant. It was a darkened alleyway, not quite what Gunner had just described as an open area, but Shar Heathrow was half his size. His stalker might be deranged, but she'd never made threats directly against him. He wasn't too worried. At the moment he was mostly excited. He might be able to end this stalker nonsense once and for all.

CHAPTER TWO

Shar Heathrow paced behind her restaurant, trying to decide how to play this. Mike Kohler was sitting at one of her tables, and Kelly, that sweet little airhead, had told him that Shar had a crush on him. She'd probably also revealed Shar had posters of him tacked all over the restaurant walls. The posters had been a joke. When her younger sister Kim caught her staring at Mike at Ally's wedding, and then Shar had refused to go introduce herself, Kim had realized Shar had a wicked crush. She'd started teasing her about him. The teasing escalated, and Kim and her husband, Colt, had come by the restaurant one time and secretly tacked up posters of Mike all over the kitchen. Shar should've taken them down, but none of the restaurant help complained about looking at Mike Kohler's handsome face, and heaven knew she enjoyed it.

Yet she couldn't just march up to him, stick out her hand, and say, "Shar Heathrow. I idolize you." It was all sports idolizing anyway, right? She'd fallen in love with football as a teenager. Her parents thought sports were idiotic. They were completely focused on their girls' talents and brains. But they couldn't say anything when Shar was elected student body vice president and had to attend every sporting event. Football was her favorite.

She'd gotten her business degree at Auburn before going on to culinary school because she always knew she wanted to start her own restaurant. Mike Kohler was the wide receiver sensation at Auburn, a football icon, winning all kinds of awards and everyone's heart with his gentle, humble manner and gorgeous face and smile. She'd never missed a home game, even streaming the away games on her computer. Of course, she hadn't met the superstar of a huge university. He was busy dating the cheerleaders. When he showed up at her sister's wedding, her confident and fun-loving personality vacated the scene, and she was too scared to even be introduced to him.

Now, he was here! At her very own restaurant. Heaven on her doorstep. She paced the alleyway, thinking up ways she could greet him and make him laugh. Should she say: "Hey handsome, sorry about Kelly. We worry she'll drown standing up in the shower." No, that was horrid of her to think, let alone verbalize. Shar loved Kelly. She was just a little perturbed with the sixteen-year-old fairy-tale believer at the moment. How about: "So glad you made it. I'd like to start with an interview before I agree to you being the father of my children." No, that was tacky too. Dang, she really wanted him ... in every which way.

"Dang, girl, why are you so pathetic?" she asked thin air.

Shar was asked on dates all the time. When she wasn't too busy with her restaurant, she even accepted some of those dates with handsome, kind, and smart men. She had fun dating. She had a great life. She didn't *need* to be such a pathetic fangirl. But come on, this was *the* Mike Kohler.

Shar faced the dumpster and jumped, bouncing from foot to foot, psyching herself up. She pretended to punch the dumpster a few times, and then yelled, "You got this, girlie!" Then her shoulders sagged, she shook her head, and muttered, "No, I absolutely have not got this." She clenched her fists and rolled her neck. "Come on, come on. Get some confidence, you pathetic loser."

"Excuse me," a deep voice said from behind her.

Shar whirled and screamed as she glimpsed a massive shadow behind her. Throwing up her fists, she yelled, "Back off if you don't want a lungful of mace!"

The man lifted his hands, palms toward her, and backed up, revealing his face as he passed under the dim overhead light.

Shar screamed again, "Oh, my, crap! Mike Kohler! Stop!"

He stopped like a deer in the headlights. He was staring at her. Mike Kohler was staring at her. She'd dreamt of this moment for a long, long time, but he wasn't staring at her like she was an amazing, accomplished, and gorgeous chef, like she usually heard from other men. He was staring like she was hoolie-hoot-oo, or translated for the layman, bat-crap crazy.

"I'm sorry," she gushed out. "I'm acting a bit nuts, and I'm not nuts ..." She paused as she thought through the past few minutes of facing the dumpster and giving herself a pep talk to meet this dream man. She was barely able to squeak out, "Okay, I probably seem a little nuts. How much did you see?"

His hands were still up as if he could ward her off. His handsome face was much too serious and those delectable lips she'd dreamt about kissing many a time were in a tight, concerned line. "Um, hey, it's good. Sometimes I ... talk to myself too."

Her heart melted. Though he didn't put off any vibes of warmth toward her, he was such a nice guy. She knew this, as she'd observed him from afar at college and through the media. He'd come from a great family. His dad was a pastor, and his mama and three younger sisters were as beautiful, kind, and supportive as anyone could hope for. Since achieving success, Mike often took his entire family on humanitarian trips and did so many great things to help the people in his hometown of Birmingham, and now in Atlanta where he lived.

"I'm sorry," she said again. "I must seem like a whack job, but I promise I'm not. Kelly humiliated me a few minutes ago by trying to set me up with you. I've idolized you for *years,* so you know how that goes. Okay, scratch that, you don't know how that goes. I mean, who would Mike Kohler possibly idolize? Anyway, things just got all awkward and squirmy inside." She showed him how she squirmed by pointing to her abdomen. His eyes flitted over her and made her hot and cold all over, but he didn't say anything.

"So, I came back here to give myself a pep talk, and all that jumping around stuff was just to pump me up to meet you. Then you obviously saw me, being all weird." She blew out a breath and wished he wasn't looking so wary of her. "I'm sorry, but I'm sure you get insane chick fans all the time. Old hat for you, right?"

"It happens," he admitted.

Shar stepped toward him, and he backed up. It hurt that he backed away, probably because he did think she was nuts, but then it struck her as so funny. He was over a foot taller than her and twice her size with all kinds of lovely muscles his t-shirt couldn't possibly hide. What did he think she was going to do to him? She started laughing. He cocked his head to the side and studied her with his eyebrows slightly lifted. Dang, he was so perfectly handsome. Seeing him up close and personal like this made her blood pressure spike, even though she was messing it all up.

"What?" she asked. "Did you think I was going to come after you?"

"Um ..."

"You did!" She started laughing harder, though she wanted to cry. This entire first meeting with her superstar crush was a disaster. Shar wasn't one to wallow in misery, so she chose to laugh. He already thought she was nuts—she might as well laugh about it. "You're like monstrous, and I'm a pipsqueak, and you think I'm going to come and take you out or something? Sorry, big guy. I left all my carving knives in the kitchen."

The look on his face made her laugh harder. He thought she was seriously disturbed. Shar had to shake this off and realize that she'd completely flubbed it up. Mike Kohler. The dream, somehow she had to let it go. Sadly, his over-the-top appeal was still there, for her, but there was no way he'd want to get to know her after this.

"Wow." She blew out a breath. "I meet the superstar of every one of my dreams, and I screw it all up." She walked to go around him. She had to get back to the restaurant and get to work, because what else could she do at this point? When she got home tonight she'd wallow in the disappointment of messing up what could've been an unreal first meeting, but right now she had to just forget about it, or she'd dissolve in a puddle of tears.

As she walked toward him, Mike backed up a couple more steps until his back hit the restaurant wall. That ticked her off. She wasn't armed and dangerous.

She planted her hands on her hips and demanded, "If you think I'm such a crack job, why'd you follow me out here anyway?"

"Well, the young redhead ..."

"Kelly," she supplied.

"She told me you ... wanted to meet me and told me you'd be out here."

She arched an eyebrow. "Do you regularly follow fans into dark alleys to 'meet them'?" So at one point, he had wanted to meet her? He sure hadn't acted like he'd wanted to meet her; he'd acted like she was insane. Which, she guessed she could give him. She had acted a little nuts.

"No," he admitted.

"Why did I get so lucky?"

"You're Ally's sister, so I figured ... you'd be safe." The look on his face didn't say he thought she was safe at all. Was the tough Mike Kohler, in reality, a wimp who was afraid of super fans? "I didn't get the chance to meet you at her and Preston's wedding, so I thought I'd come say hi. Sorry I interrupted ... whatever you were doing."

She nodded. This was going ... marginally better. At least they were having a somewhat normal conversation. Though she wished he'd followed her out here because he thought her food was fabulous or her face beautiful, but having him want to meet Ally's sister wasn't awful. Both her sisters were famous in their own rights. Ally, as the marketing genius for the Patriots and wife to wide receiver Preston Steele, and Kim, who'd been a Disney star as a teenager and was getting back into acting after taking a long break because of a stalker. Shar was prouder of her sisters than any mother; prouder than her own mother that was for sure. "I'm sorry you saw that. I was giving myself the pump-up-the-team-at-halftime-when-we're-losing-by-twenty speech."

"Oh, that's what that was." His smile slipped out, and she was the one faltering back a step. He was so incredibly irresistible, and she just wanted to freeze this moment. Those lips and sparkling dark eyes, his sculpted face and that beautiful chocolate brown skin. She wanted to squeal. Mike Kohler was smiling at her. "Well, it was nice to have met you," he said. "I'll let you get back to work."

And just like that, the dream was over. He'd obviously thought he wanted to meet her because she was Ally's sister, and who in their right mind didn't love Ally? Then he'd realized Shar needed a psychiatrist, not a date, because of the way she'd acted. So he was moving right along. Sadly, she couldn't say that she blamed him.

"Nice to meet you too," Shar murmured.

He nodded to her and strode back out of the alley. She watched him go. It was a beautiful picture, and she thought there might at least be a chance. He'd eat one of her specialties and fall in love with her cooking. After the meal was over, she could walk out and chat with him, flirt like a normal fangirl, and somewhat remedy this nightmare. There was still hope.

Her jaw dropped, and her stomach churned, when he kept walking right on. He went toward the parking lot without even glancing back at her or inhaling the tantalizing scents coming from her kitchen. She sagged against the restaurant wall for a few seconds. A few disappointed tears squeaked out. She gave herself a ten-count, and then brushed the stupid tears brusquely away and headed back to the kitchen. Facing Kelly and Anna was going to bite the big one, but sometimes you won, and sometimes you lost. Tonight, Shar had failed big time.

"What did you make of that?" Mike asked as he sat in the backseat of the bulletproof Escalade. Gunner was driving, and Lily sat in shotgun. They were headed to another restaurant across the island for dinner.

"I thought she was chill when I met her at Preston and Ally's wedding, but tonight? Definitely nuts," Gunner said.

"She's funny, and I've always liked her," Lily said.

Mike hated to agree with Lily, but as he thought back over the conversation, she was funny, and he kind of liked her too. That was insane as she showed so many possibilities of being his stalker.

Gunner rolled his eyes at his wife, which earned him an elbow in the gut. "If you look past the crazy, she does have a good sense of humor. I'll give you that," Gunner said. "But I'm definitely contacting Sutton while you two get tables for dinner. There are so many red flags with that chick. We have no choice but to check her out as a suspect and put up surveillance at her restaurant and home."

"Agreed." Mike leaned back against the cushions and looked out at the illuminated beautiful homes sliding by, massive trees in their yards looking a bit eerie against the night sky.

Red flags. Lots of red flags. And he definitely wanted to stay far away from his stalker. Yet why was he so attracted to Shar Heathrow when she showed signs of being his stalker? He'd been as confused by his reaction to her beauty and the funny way she phrased things as he was by how off she came across. But there was something in her dark eyes that was appealing and very sane. If she was his stalker, would she really have made a comment about knives and said he was "the superstar of her dreams"? He didn't think so, but how did he know how a stalker would act?

It was good that Gunner was checking into her and getting Sutton on it. Yet Mike still hoped sometime this weekend he'd get to see her again. He'd never admit that to Gunner, but as Lily gave him a wink over her shoulder, he thought maybe she'd understand.

CHAPTER THREE

Shar awoke at five-thirty the next morning and headed out to the biking and running paths that crisscrossed her beautiful Hilton Head Island. You'd think, with getting home after eleven p.m., she'd be able to sleep in, but no. Her body was just wired to go, and she woke and pushed herself physically every morning. Then, she got to the restaurant by ten to start lunch, and usually worked until closing at ten, even if she wasn't scheduled to.

She ran along the beautiful path under the live oaks with Spanish moss dripping from them, past the famous PGA golf course and so many beautiful homes. She noticed quite a few alligators in the lagoons next to the trail, but her mind was focused on her conversation with Mike last night. She was humiliated that he'd seen her so unhinged. She tried to tell herself it didn't matter, but the pit in her stomach wouldn't disappear. Mike Kohler. Her dream man had come to talk to her in reality. And she'd completely messed it up.

She saw a runner coming the other direction. There were often runners and bikers along these trails, but it was usually pretty quiet this early in the morning. The person coming was tall and built. She felt a little twinge of worry and fingered the pepper spray in her pocket. The man got closer, and in the pre-dawn light, she could see smooth, brown skin in a tank top and shorts, and the most handsome face on the planet. Mike Kohler. Her heart leaped with excitement, even as she told herself she should just stay away and not push him toward nominating her for the asylum. Did they even have asylums any more, or was that politically incorrect? Hmm. She'd have to Google that.

Mike's gaze met hers, and he blinked in surprise. Slowing, he stopped in front of her. "Hey," he said softly.

"Oh, hey." She wanted to say something funny but didn't want to scare him away again.

He tilted his chin at her and gave a very forced smile. "These trails are great."

"Yeah. I'm a lucky duck getting to live here and run the trails or the beach every morning. Show off my superhuman speed." She pumped her eyebrows. "I'm faster than Dash. You know, from the Incredibles?"

"For sure." His smile seemed a little softer. Apparently, he at least appreciated her goofy sense of humor.

"Do you want to race?" she asked.

He actually laughed. It was a great laugh. "You do realize I run the forty in under four-forty."

"Ooh." She pursed her lips and pretended a shudder. Yes, she knew that. She knew most of his stats. "That *is* fast. Come on then, let's see it." She took off running as hard as she could. She knew he could easily catch her, and maybe he'd think she was crazy again for trying to race him, but it was super fun to banter with him, and him chasing after her would fulfill so many fantasies.

Glancing over her shoulder, she saw he was watching her with a bemused smile. She beckoned to him. "Come on! Don't make me beat you, superstar."

He pushed off then and sprinted toward her. His eyes changed quickly from laughing to concerned. "Shar!" he yelled, pointing.

Shar turned back around and realized that the path had curved, and she was flirting with the edge. The edge that went down to one of the many lagoons next to these paths, lagoons that were full of alligators.

Shar screamed and tried to correct her footing, but she was already sliding in the loose gravel down the steep incline. She could spot several alligators. One was half out of the water not far below her, and the scream caught in her throat as icy horror encased her body and seemed to seal off her vocal cords.

Mike's hand shot out and grabbed her arm, easily hauling her back up the hill. Shar scrambled for solid footing and landed back on the trail with Mike's arm wrapped around her lower back. She flung both arms around his neck and buried her face in his chest. "Big teeth, alligators, scary, bite my head off," she stuttered out, trembling as she clung to him.

Mike held her close and murmured, "It's okay. I've got you."

His strong arms around her felt so safe and secure, and the trembling gradually changed from fear of becoming an alligator's breakfast to the euphoria of him holding her close. She knew she worked too much and didn't date often, but she was certain this was an over-the-top hug. The tingly, good feelings that Mike's body infused into her as he held her had never been matched with previous manly embraces. He smelled wonderful, clean and crisp, and she wanted to just bury her head in his chest and never let go.

He stepped back first. Of course, he did, but he stared down at her with such protection and depth in his gaze, she almost fell back into the alligator-filled pond. "You're okay," he muttered.

"I didn't even get a toe, or a finger, nibbled off," she reassured him.

He chuckled, and then he was hugging her again. Wow. She'd take a near-miss with an alligator to have this kind of attention from Mike. Closing her eyes, she just hung on for as long as he'd let her.

Two people were upon them before Shar even noticed anyone approaching. Mike pulled back and then released her completely. "Oh, hey," he said.

Shar forced herself to look at the couple, and her eyes widened in surprise. "Gunner? Lily? What are you two doing here?" These were her sister's in-laws and super cool people. They traveled the world on protection details for Sutton Smith, fighting human trafficking, drug lords, and all sorts of bad dudes. Gunner was super tough, and from what Preston said, had known his entire life that his career would be military and protection. Lily, on the other hand, had ditched her famous singer dad and actress mom when she turned eighteen to live on her own. She'd learned self-defense, and when Gunner rescued her from her mom's crazy plan to kill them both, she'd convinced him to teach her how to be a security op so they could always be together. Why would they be in Hilton Head? She knew she couldn't ask because they were probably protecting someone awesome and famous. She stared at Mike. Someone awesome and famous? Could they be his bodyguards? How cool was that?

Gunner's face was much too serious, big surprise, but Lily was smiling and welcoming as always. "Hey, Shar! Crazy running into you out here. We're on a weekend getaway. Ally told us to come eat at your restaurant."

"I'd love that. Come by anytime." A weekend getaway. That made sense. Mike was famous but would someone as tough as him need bodyguards like Gunner and Lily Steele? It did seem like overkill. "Do you both know Mike Kohler?"

"Of course," Lily said. "Through Preston," she hastily added.

Gunner shook Mike's hand, and Lily gave him a brief hug.

"You two just out running?" Gunner arched an eyebrow as if they were committing a sin or something.

"We just ran into each other," Shar spoke up when Mike didn't respond besides giving Gunner a stern glance. What was that all about? "And I almost fell in that," she pointed, "and Mike saved me." She gave a shudder as a gator slid through the water.

"Wow." Lily's eyes widened. "Watch where you're going, chickee."

"I will, from now on. I challenged Mike to a sprint and wasn't paying attention."

"You challenged Mike Kohler to a sprint?" Gunner's disbelieving voice showed how mentally slow he thought she was.

"I was just trying to be funny."

Lily elbowed her husband and said, "That is funny. Remember when we first met at that lake in Idaho and I tried to beat you at running, swimming, wakeboarding, fighting." She ticked off the list on her fingers and winked at Shar. "The only thing I could beat him at was flirting."

Gunner actually smiled at his wife, and Shar liked seeing a happy side of him. The guy was way too serious and had the look of, I'm-a-military-man-and-will-kill-you-with-my-bare-hands, down to a science. He wrapped his arm around Lily and said in an undertone, "I'll let you beat me at anything."

Ah, they were so cute. Lily made Gunner soft, and Shar loved that. They stared at each for a beat, but then Gunner glanced back at Mike and Shar and stiffened.

There was an awkward pause before Lily tilted her head to the side and started walking away. Gunner didn't move with her, so she grabbed his hand. "We'd better finish our run. We'll come see you soon, Shar."

"Great. It's on the house for sure."

"Thanks."

They started off at a jog. Mike and Shar both watched them go. Gunner glanced over his shoulder at them once before they were swallowed up by the trees and a corner. The look in his eyes was full of concern. She knew Gunner was a serious guy, but he seemed a little too concerned. For her or Mike? Maybe they were Mike's bodyguards. Maybe the alligator incident bothered him. She knew a lot of people were terrified of them. Shar had gotten used to them, seeing them every day, but she didn't want to tempt fate by getting too close.

"What are the chances of us running into those two?" she mused.

Mike's eyebrows shot up. "Crazy, eh?"

"Yeah." A pause ensued, and she thought she should probably just keep running. This interaction, minus the near-miss with an alligator, was a million times better than last night. She didn't want to tempt fate and have Mike act all weirded out by her again, but at the same time, would she even see him again? There was something about being close to him that told her this was more than a crush obsession. She needed to capitalize.

"Would you want to ... run together for a while?"

"Um, well ..." She could see the indecision in his eyes, and it hurt. He still thought she was off, or maybe he simply wasn't interested in getting to know her better. "We're not going the same direction."

Shar held up her hands and rolled her eyes. "Hey, it's no skin off my rear if you don't want to be around all this fun. Your loss." Turning, she jogged down the trail, depression filling her. She'd had another shot with Mike, and once again, it had not gone well. Though she had gotten a pretty great hug out of it after her alligator incident, she'd somehow messed it all up again.

Footsteps pounded after her, and she resisted the urge to glance over her shoulder; partly because she didn't want to run into a lagoon, but also because she didn't want him to know how desperately she wanted him to come after her. Her heart leaped with joy when he ran alongside her.

"My loss, eh?" he said, gifting her with that beautiful smile.

"Definitely."

He chuckled.

They jogged along for a few seconds, and she let herself sneak a glance. He was big, and he was beautiful. "You're looking thick and fine," she said.

Mike laughed.

"No, you're supposed to respond, 'You're looking thicker and finer.'" She winked.

"I couldn't really respond with that since you're thin and fine."

She grinned. "Well, thank you, Mr. Mike Kohler, superstar extra-ordinaire."

He shook his head and laughed louder. "You're a little nuts. You know that, right?"

She laughed with him. "My sisters prefer 'spicy'."

"*Spicy?*" He drawled it out so beautifully she almost stuttered off the trail and back in with the alligators. "Hmm, I like that." He gave her a sidelong glance. "So just you, Ally, and Kim?"

"You know Kim too?"

"I watched her show years ago."

Kim was just getting back into acting in California while her husband Colt worked for the famous Sutton Smith. Maybe Shar could text Colt and see if he'd give her the inside scoop. All of Sutton's operatives she'd met were pretty closed-mouth about cases, but he could at least tell her if Gunner and Lily were truly on vacation.

"Kim's awesome," she said. "You have three sisters, right?"

He looked at her strangely and stopped running, turning to face her in the middle of the trail. "How do you know that?"

"Well, I'm kind of an obsessed fan. I thought you would've noticed that last night."

His eyebrows raised, and he muttered, "I'd better head back to my hotel."

"Oh, okay." She was strangely disappointed. "Where are you staying?"

He inclined his chin to the east, toward the ocean. "By the ocean."

So he didn't even want her to know what hotel he was staying at. She understood. He was super famous and unbelievably attractive, and she'd admitted to being an obsessed fan. Of course he didn't need another obsessed fan after him, but it still stung as she really, really liked him. Even more so, now that she'd been around him a miniscule amount of time. What she wouldn't give to spend more time with him.

"If you don't have dinner plans, come by the restaurant." She smiled. "Maybe you'll see Gunner and Lily there."

His smile was obviously tight. "Thanks. See ya." He backed away and headed the other direction. Shar stood there, watching him go: those broad shoulders, that tapered waist, the striated muscles in his calves. Whoo-ee, he *was* thick and fine. And he still thought she was a nut job. He'd said see ya, but Shar doubted very much she'd see him again. She walked up the trail toward her house on Sea Pines. Discouragement over another unfulfilling interaction with Mike Kohler made it hard to get the energy to even run. At least she would have the memory of him rescuing her and holding her close.

After he jogged away from Shar, Mike hurried past thick, interconnecting trees and around a corner of the running trail, and almost ran into Gunner and Lily. They tracked his location through the phone Gunner had given him, so of course they knew exactly where he was at all times.

Gunner eyed him sternly as Mike ran past them and continued to the hotel. Most of the time they kept their distance so no one would know Mike had a bodyguard, least of all his stalker. He hoped his stalker wasn't on the island, hadn't followed him from Atlanta. Could it possibly be Shar? He sure didn't want it to be.

They made it back to the hotel and up to their floor. Mike wanted to go shower and think about his interaction with Shar. She was far too appealing to him, and watching her almost go down into the lagoon with the alligators had made him overly protective. It made him want to stay right with her, and make sure she didn't do anything too crazy. Man, she was cute.

Gunner followed him into the suite, holding the door for Lily. Mike paced toward the balcony but then rounded on them, knowing Gunner was not happy and ready to face him head on.

"What were you thinking?" Gunner started without preamble. "She could be your stalker and you just ... go on a casual run with her, through trails where we had to stay back so she wouldn't spot us?"

Mike folded his arms across his chest. "I hired you, remember?"

"Yeah, to keep you safe. If you do stupid stuff, I can't keep you safe."

"Gunner." Lily put a hand on her husband's arm, and he immediately calmed down. "Let him talk. How are you feeling, Mike?"

Gunner wisely didn't say anything, but he did roll his eyes at the feeling comment.

"I don't think Shar could be my stalker," Mike explained.

"You don't know that," Gunner thrust out. "You're telling me she doesn't act ... completely nuts most of the time? And there's still the matter of posters of you hanging all over her restaurant kitchen."

Mike clenched a fist. He knew nothing about stalkers and their behavior. Yet Shar Heathrow was so beautiful, funny, and genuine to him. Could a woman with a face like an angel: smooth skin, deep brown sparkling eyes, beautiful full mouth, and a cute dimple to boot, really be dangerous? He just didn't think she had it in her.

"What have Sutton's researchers found out?" he asked, knowing Gunner wouldn't care about his gut instincts.

Gunner studied the beach outside the suite's windows. "Nothing," he admitted.

"Ha!" Lily did a little shimmy dance. "You haven't even admitted that to me. Shar's clean, isn't she?"

Gunner gave his wife a slight grin. "It's a good thing you're cute." He looked like he wanted to start kissing her right then and there, but luckily for Mike, Gunner was the ultimate professional soldier. "So far they've found nothing in her background and nothing on her devices that would lead us to think she's the stalker."

"So that's good."

He shrugged. "I just can't get over how out there she acted last night."

Mike acknowledged that with a nod. She had acted nuts, and she admitted she was an obsessed fan, but the fact was, he liked her, and without this stupid stalker business, he'd be pursuing Shar Heathrow, hard.

Gunner's phone buzzed. He glanced at it and muttered, "Ally."

"As in Shar's sister?" Mike asked.

He nodded.

"Maybe she'd have some insight."

"I'm not asking her." Gunner pulled out his phone and slid it open. "Hey, sis," he said.

He paused and didn't talk much besides some ums, grunts, and murmurs of consent, but his jaw grew tighter and tighter. Lily arched her eyebrows at Mike, obviously as curious as he was. Shar's sister. He'd been impressed with Ally the few times he'd met her with Preston. Those two had an interesting background as they'd fallen in love when stranded on an island by drug dealers who were trying to get back at Gunner. To hear Ally tell the story, the only hard part was the poisonous snakes.

Mike wished he could ask Ally questions about her sister, but he agreed with Gunner about not asking her. Ally was feisty. Accusing her sister of being a stalker would not go over well.

He thought about Shar saying, "My sisters prefer spicy." She was far too funny and cute to him. He prayed she wasn't his stalker, but then if she wasn't, the stalker was still at large, and he couldn't date anyone anyway. So he still couldn't be with Shar. Dang.

Gunner finally muttered, "Fine, see you tonight," and hung up. He pocketed his phone, blew out a breath, and focused on his wife. "So apparently Shar talked to Ally a few minutes ago and told them we were here."

"Okay?" Lily's face was leery, very unlike her usual happy expression.

"They figured since Preston has a bye week, they'll come out for the rest of the weekend."

Mike didn't see this as too bad, but Gunner obviously did.

Maybe with Ally and Preston here, he'd get the chance to be around Shar some more and see if they had anything between them. As long as she wasn't his stalker.

"So we're meeting them at Shar's restaurant at seven tonight."

"One big, happy party." Lily gave two thumbs up, but the look in her blue eyes was very concerned. "So, if Shar is the stalker, we all get poisoned and die?"

Gunner laughed at that and pulled her into his side with an arm around her waist. "There's absolutely no history of anyone getting sick from Shar's restaurant, so I think we're safe."

Lily arched her muscular shoulders. "I'm going to order the exact same thing as Ally, and then switch our plates." She smiled and nodded. "No way would she poison her own sister."

Gunner chuckled at that. "Good plan." He glanced at Mike. "You don't have to come with us. You can stay here, order room service. We'll get the scoop on Shar and see if she's the stalker or not. This could really be a good thing."

Mike shook his head. It was bad enough he had to be away from football. He wasn't going to miss out on a chance to be with one of his teammates and friends, or seeing Shar. "The stalker has never threatened me. I'm coming with you. With Preston there, it won't look like you're my protection. I'll text him, and you know he'll invite me." And for once he wouldn't have to eat alone.

Gunner groaned. "One big, happy family."

Mike smiled. He was going to get to be around Shar more. *Please don't let her be my stalker,* he prayed.

CHAPTER FOUR

Shar was excited as she rushed from the prepping station to the grill to the oven that night. Her sister was coming to see her, and maybe Preston being around would mean more interaction with Mike. The two were teammates and decently-close friends. Mike had been at their wedding. The first time Ally and Preston had met, Mike and Preston had been together at a party at Bucky Buchanan's. Didn't that just shout bosom buddies?

Please, please let him come eat, she thought as she plated a crab meal and called to Anna that the order was up.

"Shar!" The delighted yell came from behind her. Shar whipped around, and there she was. Her twin sister, one of her favorite people in the world.

"Ally!" She rushed to her and hugged her tight. Ally was soft and curvy and exquisitely gorgeous. When people said they looked just alike, it made Shar happy. She must be an uncommon beauty if she looked anything like Ally.

Ally hugged her and then pulled back, grinning. "Hey, my spicy sis, please say you'll cook my dinner to perfection and then shut down the restaurant so you can spend quality time with me. I know you can never get enough."

Shar laughed. "Your dinner will be perfection, and I do have lots of help tonight since its Saturday, so I might get a break to talk to you."

"Ah, but I need more time with you." Ally's lips drooped.

"Okay, okay. Honest truth. I've got someone else shutting down tonight, so I can leave with you. We can stay up late talking since the restaurant is closed tomorrow."

"Better."

"Take it or leave it."

"I'll take it. I told Preston only I could come into the kitchen, but it was really because I wanted to talk to you alone." She lowered her voice. "Mike Kohler is with us." She glanced around at the posters, pumping her eyebrows. "Dream man, baby."

Shar bit at her lip and admitted, "I met him yesterday."

"And ... he's a stud, right?"

"He's amazing, but I may or may not have acted a little ... certifiably insane."

Ally laughed. "You are super funny when you do that."

Shar groaned. "I don't know if Mike agreed. Oh, Ally, I just want him so much."

Kelly rushed up to them. "I heard that! You love him, and he's here again."

"Down low," Shar begged. "Keep it chill."

"Okay, okay." Kelly grinned. "Hi, Shar's twin." Then she rushed off to respond to the beeping fryer.

Shar loved that her restaurant had the laidback feel of the beach while serving superb food, but sometimes, she and her employees were a little too relaxed.

"You'll come out and hang with us?"

"Let me cook your food to perfection and then I'll come say hi."

"Well, that's half of what I ask." She winked, squeezed her arm, and pointed at a poster on the wall. "*Mike Kohler in the flesh*," she mouthed with exaggeration then walked back out into the restaurant.

Shar laughed. She probably needed to take those down. She couldn't imagine what Mike would think if he saw them. But right now, she needed to cook. Her stomach fluttered with excitement. Mike was here. With her sister's group. She was going to wow him with her cooking, and then maybe, just maybe, she might have a chance to be around him some more. She had no illusions of the famous hottie falling for her, but being the recipient of that smile was all she could ask for.

Mike settled into the wooden chair next to Preston, glad to have his friend and teammate here. There was a connection between them having fought side by side on the field that few people had. The table was chattering happily, all comfortable with each other and excited to be together. Mike found himself mostly listening, laughing at their comments, and watching those double kitchen doors for a breathtaking brunette. So far it'd just been the little redhead and blonde servers who were rushing in and out, taking their orders and bringing them drinks and appetizers. It was packed tonight, with dozens of people forming a line out near the beach trail where a hostess kept taking names and trying to work them into a seat.

Ally leaned across Preston and whispered, "Watching for someone?"

It was uncanny how much she and Shar looked alike. Ally was more rounded where Shar was leaner, but they were really close to identical.

Mike smiled at her and saw no reason to hide it. "I met your sister last night."

"And realized straight up how awesome she is?"

Now, he saw lots of reasons to hide his first impressions of Shar. If Ally found out they suspected Shar ... It would be an explosion. "She's great," he said.

Gunner caught his eye and arched one eyebrow. It made Mike uncomfortable that his protection detail was still clearly thinking Shar was nuts and possibly his stalker. He really, really didn't want her to be his stalker.

The redhead, Kelly, brought their meals, taking two trips with a huge tray to get all the food on the table. His lobster looked and smelled amazing. They all thanked the young waitress, who'd been more subdued around Mike tonight, and then the table quieted as everyone started eating. Everyone except for Lily. As Ally lifted her fork, Lily grabbed Ally's plate of shrimp scampi and switched it for hers before plunging in quickly.

"What are you doing?" Ally asked, staring at her in confusion, her fork suspended in midair.

"Yours looked better than mine." Lily focused on her plate and ignored Gunner making a laughing slash choking noise next to her. Mike could hardly contain his own laughter. Lily was hilarious, but Ally would come unhinged if she knew the reason Lily was switching her plates.

"They're the exact same meal," Ally protested.

"Aw, c'mon." Lily plunged another bite in as if the quicker she ate, the less chance Ally had of switching back. "You know your twin sister would make yours extra special."

Ally shook her head and started eating her own meal. "Lily, you are nuts sometimes."

"It's what you love about me."

Ally just rolled her eyes and speared a piece of shrimp. Mike had been breaking and savoring his lobster. It was the best lobster he'd ever had, hands down. He dipped it in the unique garlic and sea salt butter, but it didn't even need it. He may have moaned as he ate, and he forced himself to slow down and eat some of the mashed potatoes. They were so creamy and delicious that he found himself wondering if Shar Heathrow's lips were anywhere close to as delicious as her food. He thought they might be more so and felt a deep connection with Shar simply from eating the amazing food she'd prepared.

He glanced up, and Lily gave him a sly wink. Did she know how taken he was with Shar? Did she agree with him that there was no way Shar could be the stalker? He knew she'd switched plates, but he guessed she did it to make him and Gunner laugh. Not because she truly believed Shar could ever hurt anyone.

He went back to enjoying his dinner. The only thing that would make it more enjoyable was if he could see the gorgeous chef, rave over her food, and embarrass both of them. Glancing back at the double doors to the kitchen, he caught a glimpse of dark, wavy hair, smooth tanned skin, and those deep brown eyes. She met his gaze and backed away as if embarrassed to be caught staring.

He grinned broadly at her, giving her a thumbs up to show her he loved the food and hoping, hoping she'd come talk to them. She smiled back but rushed from the open doorway back into the kitchen.

Mike's shoulders sagged. He turned his focus back on the food. At least he had the mouthwatering lobster to distract him from Shar not coming to talk with him. He caught Gunner's eye. Gunner had noticed the interaction. Of course he had, Gunner didn't miss much. His protection detail looked as if he didn't approve, and as if his suspicions were stronger than ever.

"I am such a wimp. I am such a wimp," Shar muttered under her breath. She'd stepped into her office and shut the door, and luckily Kelly or Anna hadn't followed her. The two had been harping on her all night to get out there and talk to Mike. She wanted to, but she was scared. Last night, and again this morning, there'd been definite moments where he seemed to either think she was nuts or act leery of her. She didn't want to drive him away.

But it was her family out there. Well, at least Ally and Preston were her family. She shouldn't be scared to go talk to them. Straightening her spine, she pulled off her apron, fluffed her hair, put on some fresh lipstick, and stormed out of her office.

Anna was luckily out serving, but Kelly, Isabelle, and the assistant chefs all looked up. "Oh, yeah, baby," Kelly said, "She's a woman on a mission."

"Watch out," Shar threw back at her.

"It's Mike Kohler who'd better watch out." Kelly winked.

Shar nodded. "That's right." She pushed through the double doors, with Kelly's laughter following her. Striding out into the restaurant, her feet carried her much too fast to the round table with the five people she'd been discreetly peeking on all night. She stopped short before she plowed into the side of Mike's chair. Which would be a problem because she might fall onto his lap, and then who knew what she might do to him?

"Hey," she said as all eyes swung to hers. Most importantly, a pair of deep brown eyes that seemed to sear right into her. "How was dinner?"

"Fabulous," Lily gushed out. "I've never had scampi that good, and the cheesecake was unreal too. It's the scampi I'll be dreaming about though. The sauce was so creamy, yet it didn't feel too heavy. If that makes sense?"

Shar nodded. "Thanks, Lily. I'm glad you enjoyed it."

Ally pointed at Lily. "She swapped our meals, claiming you would've made mine extra special, but mine was fabulous too."

Shar laughed. Lily was a unique person. "I should do something special for my twin, but they came from the same batch, sorry Lily."

Lily just grinned and, for some reason, poked her husband in the side. "I'm not complaining. Loved it."

"Mine was amazing, as always," Preston said. "Why don't you move to Atlanta and be our personal chef?"

"Well, first off you couldn't afford me."

Preston guffawed at that.

"But it's also smarter to have your light and healthy chef. You'd have to roll onto the football field if you ate my Southern specialties every day." Shar was dying to hear what Mike thought, but also super anxious. What if he didn't enjoy her food? She might be too into her career, but cooking was her way of expressing that she cared, and if he didn't get that message, she'd know there was truly no hope for her and the superstar.

"Now, that is a worry." Preston patted his flat abs. "Good thing my wife can't cook like you."

Ally shoved him, and Preston grabbed her and pulled her in,

kissing her quick. "Lucky for me, she does many other things to perfection."

Shar loved watching them together. Ally had lacked confidence with men for most of her life. Luckily, Preston was not only smart enough to see the jewel Ally was, but also persistent enough to pursue her.

"My steak was perfect," Gunner inserted. "Thanks, Shar."

"Of course." Her eyes slid to Mike. He was grinning up at her.

"Seriously the most unreal lobster of my life. And those potatoes were better than my mama's. But don't tell her I said that," he said, leaning forward and looking deeply into her eyes as if he wanted to convey how much he had loved the meal.

Shar flushed with relief and happiness. He'd liked it. "You had to say that. It's all awkward with the chef waiting for the last person at the table to throw out an empty compliment."

Mike chuckled low and deep. Man, she loved his laugh. "There is nothing awkward about you or that gourmet meal. I loved it."

She bowed, blushing as the rest of the table seemed to be hanging on their every word, but he loved her food. Yes! "Thank you."

"Wish I could eat here every night."

"Well, sad for you, you can't. I'm closed on the Sabbath, and you'll go back to your life of luxury on Monday, right?"

"Right." He stared deeply into her eyes. "How soon are you done tonight?"

Shar's heart leaped and then raced so hard and fast she could barely catch a breath to form the words. "I can leave at any time. The rush is over, and I have two other chefs here tonight."

"Would you take a walk on the beach with me?"

"I could let you be that lucky."

"That lucky?" His finely-formed eyebrows rose.

"To spend time with me."

Ally laughed, and Shar quickly remembered they weren't alone. She'd gotten pretty lost in his gaze. Preston and Ally were grinning at the interaction. Lily had an almost ... concerned look on her face, but Gunner was glowering at the two of them.

Shar had no clue what that was all about. She took a step closer to Mike. They were doing this walk, dang it, and Gunner Steele had nothing to say about that. "It was good to see you, Lily and Gunner."

Gunner nodded, and Lily smiled. "Thank you again. Dinner was amazing."

"Anytime."

"I'll be back at the house later," she said to Ally and Preston.

"Take your time," Ally said with an obnoxious wink, seeming to forget her insistence that Shar spend every spare minute with her.

Shar's cheeks were hot as she met Mike's gaze. "I'll just go let everyone know I'm leaving, and grab my purse."

"I'll be waiting," he said in a deep, sonorous voice that promised so many things, she felt her heart beating even faster.

"Lucky you." She gave him a brave smile that she wasn't really feeling inside, waved to everyone else, and hurried to the kitchen. Tonight may just be the best night of her entire life. Kelly and Anna were going to freak out.

CHAPTER FIVE

Mike stood with the rest of the group and pulled out his wallet. He threw a couple hundred-dollar bills onto the table and noticed the other two men do the same.

"She wanted it to be on the house," Ally scolded them.

"There's no way we are not paying for all of that food," Preston shot right back. The table was covered with the remains of appetizers, dinners, desserts, and drinks.

"I know, I'm just telling you she isn't going to like it."

"Her problem, not mine," Preston said.

Ally rolled her eyes but didn't refute him. She hugged Gunner and Lily, then got to Mike. Giving him a brief squeeze, she murmured, "Be good to my sister."

"I will," Mike promised. He should probably tell her it was just a walk on the beach. He was enthralled with Shar Heathrow, but he knew from the look in Gunner's eyes that he wasn't happy about Mike encouraging anything between them. And even if Shar couldn't possibly be the stalker, there was still a stalker out there.

Ally swatted him on the butt and walked away with Preston to the parking lot. She was so funny that he couldn't help but laugh.

Gunner inclined his head toward the beach, and the three of them walked off the wooden planks of the restaurant.

"Mike?" A female voice interrupted them from leaving.

Mike spun to face her as the other two walked quietly away. "Meredith?"

His college girlfriend was looking gorgeous on the arm of a preppy-looking guy with highlighted, swoopy hair. "Hi! Imagine meeting you here. On a weekend getaway?"

He nodded. Surprised was too mild to describe running into Meredith. He'd been so relieved when he finally broke away from her, and he'd managed to avoid her most of the time when he went home to Birmingham. His family was tight with her, so occasionally, he'd had to run into her. "Bye week."

"Aw, that's great. It's so good to see you." She smiled and waved. "Well, I'm on a hot date, so ta-ta."

Mike nodded to the man, wanting to tell him he could definitely have her. He lifted a hand to Meredith and hurried onto the trail toward the beach. He found Gunner and Lily a few dozen feet away.

"Was that ... the Meredith?" Lily asked.

Mike nodded. Lily knew her stuff. She'd seen pictures of Meredith, but how had she remembered? "Yes."

Lily's eyes widened. "We'll call it in and see what she's doing here."

"I don't like this at all," Gunner started. "Meredith here. You alone with Shar."

"You can easily follow us, and we both know how unlikely it is that Shar could be the stalker." He kept one eye on the restaurant so he wouldn't miss Shar when she walked back out. Seeing Meredith had unnerved him. She was still his number one vote for the stalker, but she'd seemed fine and more interested in her date than him. It was a little odd the guy hadn't recognized him or said anything.

"Do we?" Gunner challenged him.

Lily smiled up at her husband. "We'll head north on the sand a little bit then turn around and watch for you. You walk south, and we'll keep you in our sights. It'll be fine, and we'll get Sutton's guys all over what Meredith is up to."

"Thanks, Lily."

Gunner looked like he wanted to argue, but Shar walked out of the double doors from the kitchen. Mike instinctively started toward her, done with Gunner's protests. She looked so beautiful in a simple white t-shirt and black shorts, with her dark hair up in a ponytail, showcasing her smooth neck. Her eyes darted around hopefully but then filled with disappointment. He had to be careful, so Meredith didn't see him with Shar. He could see Meredith and her date across the open-air restaurant. Her back was to him, and they both had their menus open. Keeping one eye on Meredith, Mike strode faster toward Shar. He couldn't stand for her to think he'd ditched out on her. Gunner might have reservations, but he didn't. This walk on the beach was going to be amazing.

———————

Shar said goodbye to her employees, thanking John, her senior assistant chef for closing up tonight. Usually, she was there until close even if she wasn't scheduled to be, but the assistant chefs didn't say anything. The teenagers, Kelly and Anna, had plenty to say.

"Where you going with that *stu-ud?*"

"You gonna kiss Mike Kohler?"

"Can I watch?"

"Oh my goodness, he's so hot!"

Shar opened her hand and flapped it open and closed. "This is what you're doing." Then, she slapped her fingers together and clenched them tightly. "This is what I need."

"Ha!" Kelly laughed. "You're just embarrassed because I'm right. You lo-ove Mike Kohler. You're going to date him. You're going to *kiss* him," she said in a sing-song voice.

"Oh, stop." Shar laughed and slung her purse across her chest, so it was secure. "See you next Friday night." Kelly and Anna were great little employees, but they were also high school students and involved in school. Weekdays at the restaurant during the fall weren't busy, so it worked out perfectly to have them be her waitresses and bussers on the weekend afternoons or nights that they could fit in.

She walked out into the restaurant. It was finally starting to slow down. Weekends were always busy, but usually, fall and spring were slower. In the winter, she was only open on Friday and Saturday evenings for locals and the few vacationers who liked quiet, cooler beach time. Her eyes darted around for the group, but only their dishes on the table remained. Disappointment laced through her. Why had Mike asked her to go on a walk and then ditched her?

She glanced at the table, seeing bills fluttering in the slight breeze. Her eyes widened. Large bills. She counted six hundred dollars. She'd told them it was on the house. Even if she'd charged them, the total would've been under two hundred dollars. She was highly successful with her restaurant, and she could afford to spoil her family and friends. She was going to have words with Preston and Gunner, but Mike ... did he think he could just buy her off, and she would be so happy with the money, she wouldn't care that he'd ditched her?

A large person strode from the beach trail, stopping close to the restaurant. Shar's eyes fixed on him, and she sighed. Mike. She forgot all about her frustration over the money and drank in the sight of him as he motioned to her. She was powerless to resist any invitations from him, and she hurried across the wooden planks of the restaurant floor, toward him. He smiled and put a hand on her back, escorting her away from the restaurant before he stopped and turned toward her. A tentative smile crossed his handsome face. He was so tall and manly. She felt dainty and petite being near him. She liked it.

"Hey," he said.

"I thought you'd ditched me," she blurted out.

"No," he said quickly. "No, I just walked out on the beach for a bit while I waited for you."

She smiled, relief almost as strong as her attraction to him rushed over her. After the impression she'd made last night, she never would've imagined that he would be waiting for her. So they could walk on the beach. Nerves and joy assaulted her as he extended his hand. Placing her hand in his, she felt the rightness of his large palm enclosing over her own. This was a man who would protect and love. Could there ever be a world where the man she idolized would honestly be interested in her?

They walked slowly down the trail to the beach.

"Thanks again for dinner," Mike said. "It was amazing."

Shar stopped on the trail before they got to the sand. Dinner. "It was supposed to be my treat. You guys shouldn't have left so much money."

Mike shrugged, and those shoulders looked so tough, she wanted to touch one of them. "Sorry, we couldn't not pay for all that delicious food."

Shar started walking again. "Well, next time you'd better keep your money in your pocket."

Mike stared down at her. They left the path and squished into the sand. "Is there going to be a next time?" he asked.

Shar bit at her lip and tilted her head up to him. She squeezed his hand and couldn't even find it in her to tease. "I hope so."

Mike grinned and clasped her hand tighter. "Me too."

They walked through the soft sand and down toward the water where the sand was packed harder. Lights from houses and hotels blinked from their right, and a pale moon reflected off the endless waves to their left.

"You're lucky to live here."

"Yeah, I am." Though for the past couple of years, luck had had nothing to do with it as she'd worked her tail off to start her own restaurant.

"How long have you lived here?"

"Two years. Right after I graduated from culinary school, I found the restaurant. It was run down, and the owner was ready to give up, so I got a loan with a little help from my parents, and worked my butt off." She still worked hard every day. Her restaurant was doing awesome, and she'd been able to pay her parents back, pay down her loan every month, and had a fat savings account. She was hoping to pay off her loan in the next couple of years and buy one of the houses in her neighborhood of Sea Pines, instead of renting.

"That's great. Where'd you go to school?"

"Atlanta Culinary Art School, but I finished my undergrad at Auburn first."

His head whipped down toward her. "What? That's where I went."

"I know," she murmured.

"Four years ago?" he asked. "We would've been there at the same time."

"We were."

Mike released her hand and stared down at her. The look in his eyes was conflicted. As if he was interested in her yet wary of her. She supposed as famous and wealthy as he was, he'd have to be leery around women.

She jutted out her chin and folded her arms across her chest. If he was going to be all scared of her, she was going to call him out. "I told you I was an obsessed fangirl. What are you going to do about it?"

Mike took an obvious step back. "You've been obsessed with me since college?"

Shar rolled her eyes, her insides churning. Every time they were together, she seemed to mess it all up. But at the same time, why was he so sensitive? I mean, besides being an ultra-handsome superstar sensation, he was nothing special. "You want to make something of it?"

Mike gave a chortled laugh, but then he shook his head and gestured back toward the restaurant and parking lot. "We'd better go."

"No." Shar surprised herself by saying. "Why do you keep acting like I'm going to attack you or something?"

Mike's eyebrows lifted. He folded his arms across his chest.

"Why do you keep acting so ... fangirl obsessive with me? I'm just a regular guy, Shar."

"There's nothing regular about you. Buck up and realize you're a superstar stud who's so stinking handsome, every woman wants you." Nothing like revealing exactly how much she wanted him.

Mike looked away from her, gazing at the waves rolling in. "I'd like to actually go on a walk on a beach and just be normal for once."

Shar felt a pang. She knew Kim had struggled with being famous, and it wasn't all peaches. Her sister had had a stalker for years, and Shar knew how unsafe she'd felt. Mike was so big and strong, and she couldn't imagine anything scaring him, but all the unwanted attention would have to get old.

She nodded her understanding. "That would be tough. Are you afraid women are only after you for your fame, money, and athletic prowess?"

He inclined his chin, shrugging.

"Well, I've got news for you, superstar."

He gave her a challenging look. "What's that?"

"I'm pretty sure women are after you because you're stinking hot, an incredibly nice guy, and fun to banter with."

Mike finally smiled at her. "Really? Is that why you're after me?"

She grinned back at him but said flippantly. "Naw, it's all about you having over fifteen hundred receiving yards last season."

Mike chuckled. "You really do like football."

"I was more stoked than Ally when she married Preston."

"What?"

"I knew I'd get tickets to the games. Huge Patriots fan."

He laughed louder. "Somehow, I doubt you were 'more stoked than Ally' about their marriage."

"You're right. She's pretty gone over the guy."

Her phone rang in her purse and chirped, "Ally Steele. Prettiest twin sister on the planet." She ignored it and smiled at Mike. She wasn't interrupting this conversation for anything, even her sister.

Mike's phone rang too, but she couldn't hear who it was, or maybe he didn't have voice alerts on his phone. Her phone was still ringing and seemed shrill in the peaceful night. Suddenly, two people were walking quickly up to them. Shar wasn't the nervous type, but the way these two were deliberately coming straight at them in the semi-dark on a deserted beach, was a little unnerving. She backed into Mike. He put an arm around her and turned to face whoever was coming.

She squinted at the couple in the semi-dark, finally recognizing them as her phone fell silent for a minute. "Gunner? Lily?"

Neither of them was smiling. "We've got to go," Gunner said shortly. He gestured with his chin, and Mike turned Shar with his arm and hurried her back toward the parking lot.

"What's going on?" Shar asked. She wasn't complaining about being held close to Mike's side, but Gunner and Lily were scaring her. She peeked over her shoulder at the two of them, grim-faced and taking up the rear.

Nobody said anything as they all hurried past her restaurant and loaded into an Escalade that looked like it was built like a tank. Shar's phone started ringing again, but she quickly hit the button for *Can I call you later?* They drove west away from the ocean and toward the middle of the island. Ally responded quickly with, *Come home. Right now.*

"What's going on?" Shar repeated. They were scaring her, and Ally's text didn't help.

"We need to talk to you," Gunner said shortly, driving the vehicle with a tight grip. He turned into her neighborhood.

Shar sent Ally a quick, *Ok*, and looked at Mike. He was studying his hands.

"Are Gunner and Lily ... your protection?"

Mike glanced at her and nodded shortly. "Yeah."

"I know you're famous, but do you really need two of Sutton Smith's operatives to protect you? That'd be a bit of an overkill for the President." She smiled to show she was teasing.

Mike's jaw was tight, and nobody returned her smile or laughed at her joke. Mike opened his mouth to respond, but Gunner cut him off. "We'll talk about it inside."

Shar's body felt tight and uncomfortable. What was Gunner's deal? She knew he was a hard-nosed, military, muscle head, but when she'd met him and Lily at Preston and Ally's wedding, she'd really liked both of them. Since seeing them here on her island,

Gunner had acted very offish with her. Now it felt like they were in the middle of some spy movie. She'd rather rewind to the beach where she was looking into Mike's eyes. One glance at Mike's tight posture told her it wasn't going to be happening anytime soon.

CHAPTER SIX

They pulled into the driveway of Shar's rented house. She loved it here, with the huge Spanish oaks decorating the small yard and a running trail right out her back windows. The exterior lights were blazing, but it was darker inside the house with blinds shut that she'd never closed before. She walked up to the door with Mike by her side, Gunner and Lily taking up the rear again.

The door burst open, and Ally ushered them inside. She clasped Shar to her and muttered, "Don't worry. I'll kick all of their butts for you, especially Gunner's." She shot her brother-in-law a dark look.

Shar wasn't sure why Ally would need to kick anyone's butts for her. She said, "You do realize Gunner and Lily work for Sutton Smith and are highly trained?"

"I don't care. I'll smash them like a bug, separately, or at the same time."

"They're not only superhero material," Shar felt it her duty to point out, "they're also your brother and sister-in-law."

Ally glared at Gunner and Lily. Gunner looked defiant. Lily looked apprehensive. Gunner pointed to the open living area as if they should march in line to their lecture.

Usually, Shar had all the retractable blinds up to let in the sunshine and the great view of trees and the lagoon. Tonight, those blinds were all closed tight, and only a few lamps were on.

"We can turn on more light," she said.

"Please don't," Gunner muttered.

Shar raised her eyebrows but didn't comment. She followed the group into the living room and sat on the camel leather couch. Mike sat on her right, Ally on her left. Preston stood next to Ally, and Gunner and Lily stood across from them.

"You can sit." She gestured to the floral chairs. They weren't as comfortable as the couch, but she'd love for those two to relax a little bit. What was going on?

"I'll stand," Lily said.

Gunner nodded.

Shar stared at the two of them. Then her gaze swung to Mike. She whispered, "What's with the: I'm such a superstar, I need two highly-trained operatives to make everyone around me uncomfortable?"

Mike smiled at her attempt at humor, but then his eyes filled with a longing look. It was almost as if the brief moments they'd shared together were all she was going to get, and whatever was upsetting Ally so much was going to rip them apart.

"Do you want to start, or should I?" Ally demanded, folding her arms defiantly across her chest and glaring at Gunner.

Gunner gestured to her. "Be my guest."

Ally turned to Shar and clasped her hand. "Colt called me as we were getting settled in the guest room."

"Okay."

"Preston had found it interesting that Gunner and Lily were here, as they rarely take vacations and prefer to work in South America fighting drug lords and trafficking rings. He mentioned something about it to Colt when they were texting about fantasy football this morning, and Colt looked into it. Preston came across some intel that was apparently supposed to be kept from him." Her lips thinned, and she glared at Gunner.

Gunner didn't even look upset or embarrassed like Ally was obviously trying to make him. He arched an eyebrow and said, "Many cases are secretive to protect the client."

"Not when those cases involve my sister!" Ally roared at him.

Shar jerked back and hit the cushions. "What do you mean involve my sister? Is Kim in trouble?" Colt had saved her from her stalker over a year ago. "Her stalker isn't out of prison, is he?" Her palms got sweaty at the very thought. Kim had been through so much. She deserved a moment of peace with her husband, pursuing her dreams of acting again.

"Not Kim," Shar muttered.

Mike suddenly grasped her hand, and she focused on him. "This is all about me, Shar. I have a stalker. She's been after me since college. She threatens any woman I date. The threats have become more sinister and frequent, accidents happening to some of the women. So I hired Gunner and Lily to protect me, and I stopped dating."

He took a breath and she realized the problem. They couldn't date until the stalker was caught. Well, that stunk.

"Gunner and Lily being my protection has been ideal," he continued, "because they still have to keep their distance most of the time, but I know and trust them. And it's not out of line for me to be seen with them since I know them personally through Preston, so no one suspects I've got bodyguards."

"Oh, Mike." Shar's stomach filled with lead. She knew how challenging and terrifying something like that could be, even for someone as confident and tough as Mike. "I'm sorry you've had to deal with that."

He smiled at her.

Compassion swelled in her, but the rest of the room was deadly quiet, except for Ally who was pushing out huffy breaths next to her.

Shar bit at her lip, remembering last night. "That's why you were uncomfortable with me last night when I was acting so crazy."

"You're okay with them thinking *you're* the stalker?" Ally exploded.

Shar's head whipped from Ally to Gunner, then back to Mike. "I was ... just thinking I made him uncomfortable because he was dealing with a crazy obsessed fan." It hit her so hard, and she had to pull her hand free of his and face him square on. "You don't really ... think I'm your stalker?"

Mike looked miserable. "I, well, we ..." He lifted both palms up. "You have posters of me on your restaurant walls. You admitted to being an obsessive fan. You acted pretty nuts when I followed you behind your restaurant last night."

Everyone seemed to be holding their breath. Shar thought she should be angry or defensive, but she mostly just felt sad. She thought Mike was amazing. She had since college. He thought she was capable of being a stalker, of threatening other women who dated him. That stunk. Any dreams of dating him imploded at that moment. She didn't care how cool and good-looking he was. She could never be with someone who would suspect her of being deranged. Someone who would suspect her of ruining their life like Kim's had been for a decade.

"Aren't you ticked?" Ally asked.

Shar swallowed hard, angled her body away from Mike's, and said quietly, "More humiliated. It hurts that Mike, Gunner, or Lily could think this of me."

"Shar." Mike's deep voice washed over her, but she was too frustrated to look at him.

Ally's dark eyes flared. "Well, I'm ticked enough for the both of us!" She pushed to her feet and strode toward Gunner. "How could you?" she demanded. "How could you ever dare think that of *my* sister? It is bad enough Mike suspected her, but he doesn't even know her and barely knows me. You and I are family, you, you," she sputtered then started rattling off, "pompous, dipwad, piece of hud, supercilious, musclehead loser who thinks he knows it all."

Gunner didn't say anything, simply raised an eyebrow and looked intimidating and tough as ever. Shar knew a Steele brother would never hurt a lady, but Gunner wasn't going to back down to Ally either. It was clear he was unrepentant about doing his job and thought she was being silly and dramatic.

Lily stepped in front of Gunner and glared at Ally. "Don't you dare call my husband names."

"I'll call the jerk bait anything I want to."

"Then you'd better be ready to take me on." Lily thrust her chin out and clenched her fists. She was a few inches taller than the petite Ally and carved with lean muscle, and Shar had heard how highly trained she was. The woman took down drug lords all on her own. If Ally kept trying to pick a fight, Lily would definitely finish it. Shar loved her sister for trying to defend her, but she needed to calm down.

Preston rushed over to his wife, plucked her off the ground and carried her back to the couch. He settled onto the cushion next to Shar, with Ally straining to get free. "Let me at her," Ally yelled. "Nobody claims my twin is a stalker and gets away with it. I'll take them both down. Sutton Smith's operatives. Ha!"

Gunner appeared very amused, and Lily was still standing in front of him, looking like she would take on anybody who put her husband down. It was interesting as Shar had usually seen Lily being a soothing, calming force for her husband. Obviously, when she got riled up, she could kick some rear, and calling her husband names had riled her up. It was also interesting that Preston hadn't interceded until Lily had threatened Ally. He knew Gunner would never hurt his wife, no matter how she insulted him.

"Calm down, love," Preston was saying, "They're just doing their job. Nobody thinks Shar is a stalker."

"That's not what Colt said," she growled, straining to get free but not able to even budge from Preston's muscular embrace.

Gunner stepped up to Lily's side and took his wife's hand. He tilted his chin down to her and gave her a look of such love and devotion that Shar felt like she was intruding on their privacy by seeing it. She thought it was impressive that the tough Gunner would let Lily stand up for him.

He broke his concentration on his wife and asked Ally, "Do you want to calm down and listen for a minute?"

"No!" she shot back at him. "I want to pummel your smug face."

"Try it," Lily said.

Preston cradled her close. "Ally, love, please stop. Gunner and Lily wouldn't do anything to hurt Shar."

"Oh, right, they wouldn't. There's a stalker out there." She pointed out the windows. "A stalker who goes after the women Mike likes. Obviously, Mike likes Shar."

Shar blushed and glanced quickly at Mike. The look in his eyes said he did like her, but she was still feeling pretty dejected. He thought she was his stalker? She didn't care what Gunner and Lily thought, not really. Their job was to protect and watch for suspects. Of course, they would think everyone was armed and dangerous, but for Mike to think that way? Why couldn't he have seen that she was an obsessive fangirl, but she could never possibly hurt him, or a woman he dated? Even if the thought of him dating other women filled her with jealousy.

"They should've been protecting Shar," Ally continued. "Not suspecting her."

"You're right," Gunner said.

Every eye whipped to him.

Gunner swallowed hard and shook his head, but then he said in a quiet, clear voice. "I was in the wrong, Ally. Family is the most important thing, and sometimes, I forget that. When Lily and I are on the job, we have to put the people we're protecting first, even when it rips me apart to not focus on protecting Lily."

Lily wrinkled her nose at him, but her soft gaze showed how much she loved him and how hard their job must be at times. "Lucky for you, I can best anybody."

"Yes, you can love." He smiled softly at her before turning back to Ally. "When you and Preston got kidnapped and stranded on that island." He cleared his throat before he continued, "It was all my fault, but you never blamed me. I've always appreciated the generosity that is inherent in you. It's impressive that now, when you're defending your sister, is when you blame me. I admire your loyalty to family, and I apologize for instinctively putting my job first."

"Aw, love," Lily murmured, giving him a quick hug. "You're such a big old stud."

Ally inclined her chin. She'd stopped fighting Preston when Gunner started his speech. Her husband still held her on his lap, and she made no move to leave his embrace. "I didn't know the great Gunner Steele could ever admit to being wrong."

Lily's good humor returned. "I'm with you on that one." Then her voice became serious once more. "I never had a family growing up, Ally, at least not one that cared about me beyond using me to further their ambitions. I also think it's impressive how loyal you are, and I promise I will try to be a better sister-in-law."

Ally gave Lily a tremulous smile. "Thank you. Sorry, I threatened to kick your butt."

Lily smiled. "You scared me for a minute."

Everyone laughed at that.

Gunner gave Lily a look full of such love, and Shar felt immense jealousy that she would never have a relationship like these four had. The former SEAL turned back to Ally. "I have surveillance on Shar's restaurant and this house. I would've protected Shar if anyone came after her. You have to believe that."

Ally stared at him as if gauging his sincerity. She finally nodded. "I know you would have. I'm sorry I got all over your back. It peeved me that you could suspect Shar. She's so good, and she's always been there for me. There's no one with a heart of gold like Shar. I wish you would've asked me."

Shar adored her sister. All this talk about family. She wasn't super close to her parents, but they were good people who cared about her. She knew she was very blessed to have two amazing and loyal sisters, who were also her best friends. Mike shifted next to her, but she didn't let herself glance at the superstar, didn't let herself want more from him than he could give. Even if he was interested in her, he had a dangerous stalker who went after women he liked. That was ... disturbing.

Gunner and Lily both nodded. Gunner escorted Lily to a chair and sat down next to her. Shar was glad everyone was finally relaxing, but she was still feeling the pain of Mike suspecting her. He sat stiffly by her side and didn't say anything.

"You're right," Lily said to Ally. "We should've trusted you and talked with you rather than using Sutton's channels to research Shar."

"You've been researching me?" Shar edged closer to Ally and Preston and farther away from Mike. She felt dirty, like she was a criminal or something.

Lily nodded.

Mike put his hand on her arm. Shar felt the heat of his touch and wanted to be humble and forgiving, but she was still uncomfortable. Glancing at him, she waited.

"Your sister Kim had a stalker for a long time. What did it do to her?"

Shar didn't appreciate him taking this tactic, but she admitted,

"Made her quit her acting career and go into hiding in Costa Rica."

He nodded, his dark eyes begging her to understand. "It's rough, Shar. I've had a stalker since college. You admitted to worshipping me in college, you had all those posters, and you acted off when I first met you. Now that I've gotten to know you, I would never have suspected you, but honestly, I'm so sick of this stalker messing with my life, threatening women who go on one innocent date with me. I'd do a lot just to live a normal life. I'm not even sure I know what normal is any more."

Shar's heart went out to him even though she still wanted to feel hurt. Kim's stalker had messed with her head and disrupted her entire life. Mike was still playing professional football, being successful, and putting himself in the public eye all the time. Even with threats and the feeling of someone stalking him lingering over his head. She couldn't imagine.

"Logically, I understand," she said quietly, wishing everyone wasn't listening in. "But inside, it still hurts. I know exactly what Kim's stalker did to her and to imagine I could try to mess you up like that ..."

His eyes had such a meaningful, longing look in them that it made her heart race. He ran his fingers down her arm and then wrapped his hand around hers. Shar's body seemed to light up from his touch, and him staring at her as if ... as if she were his world. Mike Kohler. Forget all the stalker business and the accusations and the hurt. Mike Kohler was holding her hand and staring deeply into her eyes. That was all that mattered for a moment or two.

"I can understand why you'd feel that way." His voice deepened and got quieter as if he didn't want to be overheard either, but there was little chance of that with how quiet the room was. "Can you give me a chance to prove I would never hurt you intentionally?"

Shar swallowed hard and said flippantly, because it was all getting much too serious for her, "I might let you audition for the part of my boyfriend."

He chuckled, but Ally was shaking her head so quickly that Shar could see it out of the corner of her eye.

"No, Shar. His crazy stalker threatens women he goes out with once, and then things start happening to them: a near-miss with a car in a crosswalk, a paint can almost hitting one of their heads as they walked past a construction site, a couple of 'food poisoning instances in reputable restaurants'. And that's just the ones we know about. There could be other near-misses that the girls either didn't notice or didn't tell Mike about."

"How do you know about all of that?" Gunner pinned Preston with a look.

Preston shrugged. "Bucky confided in me."

"You can't date him," Ally continued. "Not until she's caught. I'm sorry."

Gunner nodded. "I'd have to agree with that Shar."

Mike's hand tightened around hers. Shar turned to him. They hadn't even been on a date. Their walk on the beach was the closest thing to it, and now everyone was agreeing they couldn't date. Not until a stalker who'd been after him for four years was caught.

"Would you ... have to agree as well?" she asked.

Mike's eyes swept over her face, and she now understood the longing in them. He wanted to date her, but he wouldn't put her at risk. "I can't risk anything happening to you."

The way he said it made her heart threaten to burst, but there was still the fact that he wasn't going to date her. Despair seemed to cloak the room. She glanced at Gunner. "How long have you been on the case?"

"A couple of weeks. We're just getting started and we'll find her, Shar." He cracked a grin, which was rare for Gunner. "And then you can let Mike audition for the part of your boyfriend."

Lily winked. "Y'all are adorable. We'll find her, Shar. I promise."

Gunner nodded to Shar and then stood as if that was the end of it. He took Lily's hand and said, "Shar, we'll keep an eye on you and the restaurant. If you feel worried at all, you call me."

"Thanks, Gunner." She prayed she wasn't a target now from one innocent walk with Mike. In her mind, they had much more between them than the walk, but hopefully, the stalker didn't know that.

"Mike, we'll meet you out front." He turned to Preston. "Would you and Ally walk with us out front? I think these two need a minute."

Preston stood with Ally still in his arms and set her on her feet. "Sure."

Ally squeezed Shar's arm as they walked past. "We'll be right back."

The two couples walked outside, talking about the boys' little sister, Lottie. It seemed all was well with the Steele family, despite Ally coming unhinged, calling Gunner a lot of names, and Lily threatening to take her out. Shar hoped all was well with her and Mike, but even if it was he still had to leave her.

CHAPTER SEVEN

As soon as the front door closed, Mike turned to Shar on the couch, still holding on to her hand. "I want to apologize again, for even suspecting you."

Shar shook her head. "Thanks for bringing Kim into it. That helps me understand how hard it would be and how desperate you would be to catch her. Have you had other protection?"

He nodded. "My family hired private investigators initially, then as soon as I got with the Patriots, Bucky Buchanan, the owner, hired bodyguards and investigators, but nobody's found anything. When Preston suggested Gunner and Lily would help me, I reached out to them at Preston's wedding, but they had to finish another job, so they're just getting started as Gunner said."

"They seem confident they can catch her."

Mike nodded. "They're good. I'm hopeful they can end this."

Silence fell, and Shar bit at her lip. She'd gotten pretty bold with Mike about auditioning to be her boyfriend, and she wondered what he was thinking. He was a world-famous, ultra-perfect man, and she was a workaholic chef without much acclaim.

Mike released her hand, wrapped his arm around her shoulders, and drew her closer to him. Shar glanced up into his deep brown eyes, wanting to be with him, but knowing she needed to let them find the stalker first. She didn't want some deranged woman after her, though she'd take the risk to be with Mike.

"Has your stalker ever actually hurt any of the women you've dated?"

Mike studied her, his beautiful mouth pursing. "A lot of near misses."

"Then maybe it's worth the risk."

Mike smiled, but it fled quickly. "No way am I risking you." He leaned down closer to her.

Shar's body arched up toward his without conscious thought as Mike's hands urged her closer still. In one swift movement, he placed his hand under her thighs, and the other hand dropped down to her lower back. He swooped her off the couch and against his chest, holding her tightly. Shar let out a small gasp and Mike smiled.

"You were too far away," he murmured.

"Well, I'm glad you remedied that problem as now there is no space between us at all." She loved every second of feeling his strong body wrapped around her. She wrapped her right hand around his shoulder and placed her left hand on his well-built chest. His clean scent washed over her. She didn't know if it was a type of cologne or just the scent of his soap, but she loved it, so manly and fresh-smelling like pine trees after a rainstorm.

"Better," he said with a deep rumble in his voice. "Much better."

"I don't know," Shar said, running her right hand across his shoulder and his neck, cupping the back of his head and tugging his mouth closer to hers. "I can think of something that would be even better than this."

"Oh yeah?" He quirked an eyebrow at her, his breath warm on her lips. "What's that?"

"You could put my head in the clouds with that beautiful mouth of yours."

He grinned. "You like my mouth?"

"Your lips were carved by angels," she said.

Mike chuckled. "I'd better use them on an angel then."

"Aw, you big sweetie."

Mike smiled but didn't reply. Instead, he pulled her closer and pressed his lips to hers. An explosion of desire and warmth ensued. Head in the clouds was so understated that Shar was embarrassed she'd used the term. Being in heaven, experiencing the most euphoric moment of her life, knowing nothing and no one could ever compare to Mike's kisses, were closer to the truth.

Shar's arms encircled his neck, and she clung to him as their lips worked in synchrony to produce the most beautiful kissing session. The passion in his kiss was unrivaled, but then he slowly, tenderly opened her mouth with his tongue and traced it along the inside of her lips. Her mouth tingled, and all she wanted was more, more of Mike. Nonstop kissing from Mike.

She pulled back slightly, panting for air. Mike gazed down at her with eyes full of love. Was she insane? Love? They hardly even knew each other. She was just caught up in the passion of that kiss, and the insane miracle that the man she'd fantasized about for years was holding and kissing her.

Mike murmured, "Shar," in a beautiful husky tone, and she had never loved the sound of her name so much.

"Can I record you saying my name like that so I can replay it over and over again?" she asked him, hoping she hadn't just ruined the moment.

"Sure. We'll do that later." He smiled slightly, and then he was kissing her again.

Shar knew nothing and nobody could ever pull them apart. They were meant to be together, and this kiss to end all kisses was showing her the path to her life. Mike. He was the one she was meant to be with. Gunner and Lily would find that stalker, and then she and Mike could be together.

A door opened and closed, and she would've ignored it, but a throat cleared. Mike released her from the kiss but kept her securely in his arms. "Yes?" he growled, clearly perturbed. Shar had never heard him disgruntled like that, and it made her laugh.

Mike smiled at her, laughing at him, then tenderly traced his finger along her jaw. His eyes were completely focused on her.

"We've got to go," Gunner said from much too close by.

Mike rolled his eyes and lifted Shar to her feet. Standing next to her, he took her hand and faced Gunner. "If you ever interrupt me kissing Shar again, I'll fire you."

Gunner's face twitched in what might have been a smile, but he spoke rapidly. "You received an email through your fan page tonight. It had your picture on it, with a target over your face."

Mike reared back. "She's always threatened the women I date, not me."

"There was a note too, 'You claimed you loved me, but you always loved football more. Now, I'm going to kill you'."

Mike's eyes widened. He cleared his throat and said, "My ex-girl-friend always claimed I loved football more, and when I broke up with her, I used my career as my excuse."

Gunner nodded. "With you talking to Meredith Ulysses tonight, it's just all too coincidental. We're leaving now, and Sutton is sending Colt to ensure Shar stays safe."

Mike's grip on her hand tightened, and his jaw became iron. "I thought Meredith had been checked into, and Sutton's men had cleared her."

"Cleared, but some people are experts at deception." Gunner shook his head. "I don't like her randomly showing up, on the night this email comes in, and especially at Shar's restaurant. Meredith lives in Birmingham. Why would she be here?"

Mike shrugged. "She was with a guy. They looked like they were dating. She seemed better than she usually seems when I see her."

"I still don't like it. Let's go."

"Not if she's coming after Shar." Mike's hand was strong around hers. He wouldn't desert her.

Gunner's forehead wrinkled, and he seemed to be thinking. "It gets messy with family," he muttered.

Shar ignored Gunner and asked Mike, "Who's Meredith Ulysses?"

"My college girlfriend," Mike said. "She's been a suspect as the stalker, but there's no proof besides her being ticked when I broke up with her. There are so many fans who could be the stalker. It's hard to know who to pin it on."

Shar nodded her understanding but sort of commiserated with the college girlfriend. If she had Mike as her boyfriend then he dumped her, she might go insane too. She also knew how it felt to be suspected by Gunner Steele. Not fun at all. "She was at my restaurant?"

"Yeah."

"You're right, Mike." Gunner nodded decisively. "I don't like it. We're all clearing out. We'll have Preston and Ally meet Colt in Atlanta. Colt will stay with them until this is resolved, and Kim will stay at Sutton's. She'll be safe there if anyone thinks to involve her." He focused on Shar. "Pack a bag. I don't know when we'll be back."

Shar didn't move, just blinked at him. "I can't just ... leave. I've got my restaurant to run."

"I'm sorry, Shar. Hopefully, we won't be gone long, but ..." He shook his head. "Something's off, I feel it."

Shar wasn't leaving. This stalker didn't even know she and Mike liked each other. All the blinds had been closed tight when they kissed. This was overkill.

Lily burst into the room. "I sent Preston and Ally to Atlanta to meet Colt," she said quickly.

"Without even getting their stuff or saying goodbye?" Shar thought Gunner and Lily were much too intense. She didn't see her sister near enough, and they'd just sent her and her husband away?

"They'll have to get it later. Let's go," Gunner said.

"No," Shar said.

Mike glanced down at her. "We'd get to be together."

Shar smiled at that, but she knew he had responsibilities too. "You're just going to ditch out on football and go wherever Gunner tells you to go?"

Mike's brow furrowed. "I thought Shar was coming to Atlanta with us. She can stay at my house in Marietta, and you both can protect all of us."

"No," Lily said shortly. "A note just got delivered to the hotel. I was the emergency contact when you didn't answer. I had the manager send me a picture of it."

Mike looked embarrassed. "I felt it buzz in my pocket, but no way was I interrupting that kiss."

Gunner kept a straight face, but Lily's eyebrows shot up.

"What does the note say?" Gunner asked.

Lily held up the screenshot. He read it aloud, "Do you think your beautiful chef likes poison, or would she rather be burned alive? Ditch her ... unless you want to find out." It had a picture of the two of them leaving the restaurant toward the beach path. "And I just got word from Sutton. A dumpster started on fire behind your restaurant. They put it out, no worries, but ..."

Shar's stomach pitched. "Why didn't they call me?"

"The chef said it was small, and they were able to put it out. Sutton checked in with them because of the cameras Gunner had set up. Unfortunately, they didn't get any angles of the dumpster before the fire started, but you can see the glow of it burning in one of the feeds. Sutton simply told them he was from the security company that monitors the restaurant." She looked at Shar. "We'll keep those camera feeds going and get a few more installed to make sure your restaurant and home are protected."

They wouldn't dare burn her restaurant. It made her sick, but it also meant they were playing a more serious game than she'd realized.

Mike released her hand and pulled her into his side. "I can take a break from football," he said.

Shar stared up at him. "You would do that, for me?"

Mike nodded seriously.

"What do you think, Shar?" Gunner asked. "We can take you to

Atlanta to be with Colt, Preston, and Ally. Colt's one of the best, and I trust him implicitly, but I'd feel better about getting you to a safe house since you now have a target on your back. That way, Colt would only have to watch out for Preston and Ally."

Shar glanced at that note again then around at all the concerned faces, settling on Mike. It would give her time alone with him, and she definitely wouldn't feel safe knowing someone was threatening to poison or burn her or her restaurant. "Is someone following this Meredith?"

Gunner nodded. "We'll get someone on her. It seems really suspicious that she'd show up here and with the two threats, the pictures, and the fire coming in tonight."

"But what if it's not Meredith and you don't find the stalker? How long do we just hide out? And what if they burn down my restaurant?"

"We'll watch the restaurant. I'm betting if we go, they'll spend their time trying to find Mike." Gunner shrugged. "I don't know how long we'll have to hide out, but I'll keep you both safe, and Sutton's techs and field guys will work hard to find her, or him."

Mike pulled her in close, bent, and brushed his lips across her forehead. "Please come with us, Shar. I can't stand the thought of something happening to you."

Shar glanced up at him, so strong, so handsome. The thought of leaving her restaurant made her slightly panicked, but she couldn't resist the safety and excitement Mike offered, so she found herself nodding.

Mike gave her a relieved smile and a soft kiss. Shar melted against him.

Gunner interrupted, issuing orders. "Lily, take the Escalade and meet at the destination we discussed. I'll follow these two in a vehicle Sutton is sending over. Shar, go pack a bag. Mike, give her some space."

Shar rolled her eyes at Mike, who gave her one more hug before letting her go. Lily saluted Gunner mockingly. "Aye, aye, sir."

He gave her a quick kiss and a gentle nudge toward the front door. "Love you."

Shar hurried up the stairs to pack. She was deserting her house and her restaurant, but she was going to be with Mike. It was foreign to her to not take care of her responsibilities, but she didn't want to go to Atlanta or stay here. Even if she hired protection or Sutton sent someone, it would be terrifying to think a stalker was watching her. Mike and some safe house sounded like pretty good options at the moment.

CHAPTER EIGHT

Mike did not want to just up and leave his life, especially football. He chafed at the idea of missing more practice, and no way would he miss next Sunday's game, but he trusted Gunner and Lily, and he definitely wanted Shar to stay safe. Coach Warren and Bucky, the team owner, had been informed about what was going on. They were two of the few people who knew about his stalker. Ally was currently the head of marketing for the Patriots, so she'd have to figure out how to spin his absence to the press if he actually had to miss next Sunday's game. He tried to think positive. There wouldn't be an absence. If Meredith was really his stalker, Sutton's guys would find the proof they needed. If it was someone else, maybe the person who had delivered the note was caught on camera, or they could track the email address down.

They drove through the quiet night to a remote airport, then boarded a small jet and flew to Colorado. He talked quietly with

Shar, Gunner, and Lily, and tried to focus on the new Robin Hood movie someone put on for the plane ride, but his mind was stewing with his plan. He was fine with getting Shar settled here with Gunner and Lily, and making sure she was safe. Spending some time alone with her this next week wouldn't be something he would complain about, but then he was going to fly back for practice on Friday and Saturday, and be at his game on Sunday. He couldn't miss a game. It just wasn't in his makeup. Colt would be there as well as the Patriots security. The stalker had never threatened him personally, except for the random email, but famous people got emails like that often. Though he trusted Gunner's instincts, he wasn't going to uproot his entire life for them.

They were finally driving through the mountains toward the safe house. He glanced over at Shar, sitting in the bucket seat next to him in the Escalade that had been waiting for them at the private Colorado Springs airport. She'd been pretty quiet, and he wondered how she felt about her life being uprooted. She might be a huge fan of his, and they'd shared that one incredible kiss, but she probably resented having to leave her restaurant because of him.

She glanced over at him and saw him watching her in the dark interior of the vehicle.

"You okay?" he asked quietly.

"Ready to do the horizontal coma on a comfy bed. You?"

He smiled. "That does sound pretty great." The flight had been comfortable, but he hadn't been able to sleep, and it was almost three a.m. They were driving through thick woods, and it was dark enough that he couldn't see much past the dirt road and the closest trees illuminated by the headlights.

Finally, a clearing appeared, and the headlights lit up a two-story log cabin with a detached garage. Lily stayed with them in the car while Gunner did a sweep of the cabin. He came back and nodded shortly. "Clear."

They all unloaded and wearily made their way up the front porch while Gunner put the Escalade away in the garage. It was a classic cabin with a wrap-around porch. Inside, there was a large gathering area and a master suite on the main level, with a mudroom behind the open kitchen. Upstairs, there was a loft with a reading and tv nook and play area, and Mike could just see three doors at the back of the loft. Maybe bedrooms or a bathroom. There'd been a bag with clothes and toiletries for each of them in the Escalade in Colorado, except for Shar who'd been able to pack her own.

Lily headed for the master bedroom with their bags. Gunner followed her but stopped and glanced at them. "We're taking the master because it's the security center. You two okay upstairs?"

Shar nodded.

"Sure," Mike said.

"Get some rest. We're safe here."

"Thanks," Mike said.

He followed Shar up the stairs and to the three doors he'd seen. There were two bedrooms on either side of a bathroom. He'd felt pretty comfortable and awesome kissing her earlier, but she'd been so quiet throughout their travel, and he wasn't sure if she was regretting the kiss or just upset about her life being uprooted. Probably the latter, but he wasn't sure what to say.

Holding on to his bag, he turned to her. "Take your pick."

She smiled. "I'll take the one on the right."

"Any reason?" He wanted to extend their time alone together, maybe get a glimpse if she was feeling anything for him, or if his stardom status had worn off and now she wasn't a crazy fangirl, not enamored by him any longer.

"It's closer. I'm so tired I'm staggering like a drunk."

He smiled. "Closer as in three steps?"

"Yep."

So she was only tired. That made sense and didn't make him quite as concerned. She wasn't upset at him for pulling her from her life, or at least she wasn't thinking the kiss was awful. She couldn't, could she? That kiss had been unreal, and unless he was completely off, she'd been a more than willing participant.

"Goodnight."

"Night." She pushed open the door and disappeared.

Mike stood, wishing she wasn't so tired. He was tired, but he also felt frustrated, out of his element, and at the same time, so drawn to Shar. He wanted to stay up and talk with her, without Gunner and Lily right there listening in.

He forced himself to walk into his bedroom, put his bag in the closet, slip out of his clothes, and pull the covers back on the king-sized bed. At least it was king-sized. He closed his eyes but struggled to drift off, staring at the dark ceiling for what felt like hours before his eyes finally got heavy, and he fell asleep.

S un was streaming through the large windows, and he heard a strange buzzing sound. Mike felt like he'd been clobbered over the head. He groaned and rolled onto his side, reaching into the pocket of his pants heaped on the floor for his cell phone. Pushing a button to stop the buzzing, he looked at the display with bleary eyes. Brett White. An old friend. They'd known each other for years, meeting at football camps in high school, playing against each other on opposing teams in college, then both being drafted by the Patriots. Brett hadn't shone his rookie year and had been traded quickly to the Giants. He called every once in a while to chat, but Mike didn't know he had this new number. When Gunner and Lily took Mike on as a client, they'd gotten rid of his regular phone and given him this one with "scrubbed" contacts.

"'lo?" Mike grunted out.

"Dude! How are ya?"

"Tired." Mike stood and stretched, looking out the windows at the view of trees, trees, and more trees. It was green and pretty, but a little claustrophobic.

"They working you too hard?" Brett laughed. "Transfer over here, we'd love the superstar Mike Kohler on our roster." There was a bite to his voice. Mike had been afraid Brett had blamed him for being pushed off the Patriots, and now Mike was hearing rumors that he wasn't long for the Giants either, and it was doubtful if anyone else would pick him up.

"Thanks, man. I'll remember that." He tried to be upbeat.

"We're playing you in a week. You want to get together when I fly in?"

"Um ..." Would he be playing next Sunday? Everything in him said yes, but he wasn't sure what to say to Brett.

"You too busy for an old friend?" Brett jabbed at him.

"No, it's just, I'm actually out of town, for some ... family issues." He hadn't planned on having to explain, thinking how Ally would have to deal with the media, not him. He was fumbling.

"Oh, sorry to hear that. Anything I can do?"

"No, just be nice to my team next Sunday if I'm not there." He had to be there.

Brett laughed. "You can definitely not plan on that."

Mike laughed with him. "I'll let you know if plans change."

"You do that. Take care, man."

"You too." Mike slid the phone off and set it on the nightstand.

There was a hard rap on his door then it pushed open. Gunner stood there. "Who were you talking to?"

"Brett White."

Gunner's brow furrowed. "I don't remember him being in your list of approved contacts."

"I wondered that too. Should I have asked how he got the number?"

Gunner shrugged nonchalantly, but he didn't appear too happy. "He knows a lot of your teammates from being on the Patriots three years ago. He could've gotten the number fairly easily. We haven't gone to the extreme of broadcasting the news of your stalker to family, friends, or teammates, but maybe with the situation escalating as it has ..." He put his hand out. "Let me go look at the phone. Sorry, but I might need to shut it down to make sure no one can track our location."

Mike palmed the phone, walked over, and handed it to Gunner. It was a chafing kind of feeling to be a successful, full-grown man and have to follow another strong-willed man's instructions for safety. He didn't like not having a phone. He didn't think he was addicted to his phone, but he liked to read the news, his scriptures, and books on it, and he checked social media, the stock market, and the weather as much as the next person.

Gunner nodded his thanks and headed back down the stairs. Mike walked to the bathroom door. It was locked, so he leaned against the wall to wait. Shar was probably in there. He was anxious to see her this morning. Hopefully, now that she wasn't tired, she'd share her funny personality and smiles with him again. Maybe being cooped up in this forest retreat wouldn't be too bad. He and Shar could go on runs through the forest, work out together to keep him ready for the game, snuggle up on the couch, and she could read, whatever she enjoyed reading, while he studied plays. She claimed to be a huge football fan. Maybe she'd be up to watching game tapes of the Giants' defense. He was definitely going to beg her to cook some amazing delicacies for him.

The door opened, and a little steam eased out, haloing the beautiful woman in the doorframe. She had a towel wrapped around her torso that showed off her toned shoulders and shapely legs. Shar's dark hair was wet and trailing down her back. Her smooth skin was washed clean, and her dark eyes looked so big and beguiling. He took an unconscious step toward her.

She focused in on him, and her eyes swept down then up his body. She gave a little gasp and shut the door again.

Mike stood there, staring at the door. Maybe the snuggling on the couch wasn't happening. He looked down at himself. He was only wearing boxers. Shoot. Had that made her uncomfortable? As an athlete, he was pretty used to working out or walking around the locker room in minimal clothing. He hadn't thought much of walking around in boxer shorts.

Should he go slip his clothes back on so he didn't embarrass her? He stood outside the bathroom door debating what to do and hoping she'd just open it again.

———

Shar clung to the bathroom doorknob, panting for air. She'd been bleary and out of it this morning, so she'd wandered into the bathroom and showered, not thinking to grab clean clothes. When she'd opened the door and seen Mike in nothing but boxers, and realized she was in nothing but a towel, she'd slammed the door shut again. Now she had no clue what to do, and she felt stupid and immature. Mike had all manner of gorgeous women throwing themselves at him at all times. What would he think of someone like her who could barely look at his glorious chest without having heart palpitations? It wasn't that she hadn't seen a man without a shirt on before. It was that Mike was just too perfect and appealing to her.

She waited a few seconds, then squared her shoulders. She could open the door, and if he was still standing there, she'd just say good morning and slip into her bedroom. No big deal.

Easing the door open, she peeked out and about passed out. He was still standing there, in nothing but boxer shorts. Shar's eyes feasted on his muscular torso, chest, and arms covered with deep brown skin. He was so fascinating that it took a few seconds before her eyes made their way to his face. He was smirking at her.

"Morning, Shar," he murmured in his deep husky voice.

Shar almost slammed the door again. Instead, she clutched the towel to her to make sure it didn't slip off and tilted her chin imperiously. "Good morning," she managed to get out of her suddenly dry throat in a semi-confident tone.

He stepped closer, filling up the doorway and making her wonder how she was going to slip past, or if she even wanted to. What she really wanted to do was touch those lovely-looking muscles on his chest and see what they felt like.

"Any plans today?" he asked.

Shar smiled. "Nope, the schedule has been cleared." It was an odd feeling: sort of liberating but also kind of scary to have no work and no plans. She worried about her restaurant but was grateful it was off-season, knowing her staff could handle it.

"If we can talk our Nazi bodyguards into it, do you want to go on a hike through the forest?"

Her eyes flickered down to his chest again. "Maybe we should put some clothes on first."

Mike chuckled. "I can see the wisdom in that."

"Don't want poison ivy on my bare ..." She stopped herself.

Mike's eyebrows lifted, and his voice became even huskier than usual. "No, we wouldn't want that."

She started forward, but he didn't give her much space. Brushing her arm against his bare chest, she heard him pull in a quick breath. Heat flushed through her, and she hurried into her bedroom and shut the door. Hopefully, the stalker got caught soon because she had no clue how she was going to survive in such close proximity to that perfect man. Her hero-worship from college on up was being taken to new levels as she got to know him better. A hike in the woods sounded great, but kissing the day away sounded even better.

CHAPTER NINE

Shar decided to custom-make omelets with Lily and Mike chopping the veggies for her and cutting up some fruit to go with the omelets. Gunner had been checking things outside, but now he was on the phone with Sutton. Shar was anxious to hear any news. Maybe they'd get lucky and that Meredith girl's face had been picked up by the hotel's security cameras as she dropped off the note, or they could trace the email straight back to her.

She had a hard time peeling her eyes off of Mike. He'd showered quick and dressed in a white t-shirt and some black joggers. He looked so good, and he kept giving her warm glances every time their eyes met. At least they were past him suspecting her of being his stalker. She craved a lot more time alone, to get to know each other and hopefully share a few more of those delectable kisses from last night.

Gunner exited the master suite with his phone in hand. "It smells good."

"Thanks. What do you want in your omelet?" Shar asked Gunner.

"Everything."

"Exactly what everybody said. Good thing nobody's picky." Lily's omelet was already on a plate, but she was stirring up some juice and hadn't started eating yet. Shar slid Mike's omelet onto a plate and said, "Order up for Mike Kohler."

Everybody laughed.

"Thank you," Mike said, taking the plate and adding some fruit to it. He sat at the bar across from her.

Shar poured the egg mixture in then started adding all the veggies, bacon, ham, and sausage. The pantry, fridge, and freezer were all well-stocked, and that made her happy. At least she could still cook, even if she had nothing else to do but ogle Mike.

Mike sat there, watching her, not picking up his fork to eat.

"Eat while it's hot," Shar encouraged. "Lily, you should sit down and eat also."

Gunner took the orange juice from Lily and walked it over to the table. "Yes, you should eat."

"Okay," Lily said.

Mike still didn't pick up his fork.

"Mike, eat."

"No. I want to wait until yours is ready."

"Then yours will be cold. That's stupid."

Mike smiled and shrugged. "I like watching you cook, and I don't care if it's cold."

Shar rolled her eyes but thought it was very thoughtful of him. She'd cooked for a lot of people, quite often for men she dated more than a few times, and every time she told them to eat, they would listen. Mike seemed to love her food, but he was too much of a gentleman to eat without her.

Shar flipped Gunner's omelet and sprinkled cheese on it. Then, there was nothing to do but wait for it to finish cooking.

"What did Sutton say?" she asked.

Gunner folded his arms across his chest. "Quite a lot. First of all, they got ahold of your chefs and told them you'd won a getaway from the Patriots' football team and wouldn't be back for a few weeks. They were happy you were getting a vacation and promised they'd keep the restaurant going."

"Thanks." Her assistant chefs were good guys, and luckily, it was the end of September so the restaurant was not as busy as it would be in the summer months. It was still tough for her to be away from her restaurant, but her people were well-trained, and she had to keep reminding herself it wasn't going to fall to the ground without her.

She slid Gunner's omelet off and started adding egg mixture and all the meats and veggies to the pan for hers.

"Why don't we all sit down for the rest?" Gunner requested.

That didn't sound good.

Lily and Mike carried the fruit platter and their plates over to the larger dining room table. Gunner took milk, juice, cups, and silverware over, then came back for his omelet. By the time they had it all set up, Shar's omelet was flipped and covered with cheese. The silence was a little unnerving as they waited for her omelet to finish cooking. She glanced at Mike, and he pumped his eyebrows at her and gave her a smile. It seemed being away from the stalker was making him more relaxed and happy. Shar wondered what would happen when the boredom of being stuck in this cabin sunk in along with the panic of her not being at her restaurant and Mike not playing this Sunday. Yet, maybe if they could kiss the time away, they wouldn't experience any boredom or worries.

Finally, her omelet was done. She slid it onto a plate, turned the stovetop off, and followed everyone to the table. She was nervous about whatever Gunner had to tell them. It was so crazy that she hadn't even gone on a date with Mike, yet she was caught up in this mess of his stalker coming after him. Bad timing on her part? But as she sat next to Mike, and he gave her an irresistible smile, she didn't know if it was bad timing. She wanted to be close to him, and this was the perfect opportunity. As long as the stalker was caught soon and didn't harm her restaurant.

Lily offered a prayer before they all started eating. There were soft moans of approval, but besides that, silence.

Shar was chafing to know what was going on, what Sutton had said. "Can you please share the news?" she said to Gunner.

"Please, can we wait until after breakfast?" Mike asked Gunner. He swung his gaze to Shar. "This is so delicious, and I want to give each bite my full attention."

Lily held up a hand. "Yes, Shar, let me just savor this delicacy for a minute. We've got all day to focus on the dum-dum stalker."

Shar laughed. She appreciated the compliments, and she'd heard Gunner and Preston's little sister, Lottie, call them a dum-dum if they teased her.

Gunner nodded his agreement, but his mouth was full. Shar had always loved to cook, and it was even better if someone appreciated what she cooked. She took a bite and enjoyed the savory eggs, spicy meats, and flavorful vegetables. They were just simple omelets, but she was happy they enjoyed them. It was also nice to sit and eat. She rarely had a chance to do that, often scarfing down a rejected meal or throwing something easy together to eat while she worked. The omelets were good, and the view was incredible, with the sun shining through the forest outside the windows, and Mike Kohler inside the windows.

He caught her staring at him, and smiled. She blushed and looked away. What was a girl to do when the most incredible man ever was sitting feet away?

Mike and Gunner finished their omelets, and Mike caught her eye. "That was amazing. Thank you for cooking for me ... I mean for us."

She smiled. Him loving her food felt intimate and like he truly understood her.

Gunner picked at the fruit as she and Mike exchanged glances.

"I'm glad you enjoyed it," Shar said.

"It was more than enjoy. It was heaven."

Shar smiled and looked down, pleased. She was only about halfway through, and her stomach felt distended. She noticed Lily slide the last third of her omelet onto Gunner's plate. His eyes lit up, and he gave her a quick kiss before diving in.

"That was so delicious," Lily said to Shar, "But my gut was going to bust wide open if I ate all of that."

"Thank you," Shar said, "I'm with you." She turned to Mike. "Do you want the rest of mine?" It felt so intimate to be offering him half of her breakfast like they were a couple, probably because Lily had just done the same thing with her husband.

Mike leaned closer. "You would do that for me?"

"Definitely." She wanted to say something cheesy like she'd do anything for him. Instead, she said, "I can't eat anymore."

"Thank you." He pushed his plate next to hers.

Shar smiled and scooped the rest of her breakfast onto his plate. She ate a slice of ripe mango, one of her favorite tropical fruits with its sweet yet spicy flavor. It was fun watching Gunner obviously enjoy the breakfast, but it was much more intriguing to her how Mike savored her food. He caught her gaze and gave her a wink.

When Gunner finished, he patted his flat stomach. "Thank you for getting stranded in this cabin with us, Shar."

"It wasn't by choice," she shot back at him, "But you're welcome."

He nodded. "I know." Then he got right down to business. "So, the report. First of all, they were able to use the hotel's cameras to trace down the teenager who delivered the note. He said a beautiful blonde lady had paid him twenty bucks to take the envelope to the front desk. So that makes us think ...""

"Meredith," Lily filled in.

"Yeah. And the email threat was traced back to some computer geeks going to school at the University of Alabama in Birmingham where ..." He shook his head, seeming very annoyed with all of this.

"Meredith works." Mike sat up straighter.

"Who also claimed a gorgeous blonde paid them to set up the accounts."

"So, the police question this Meredith." Shar didn't see the problem, and it seemed they had found their person. They'd be back home by tonight. She snuck another glance at Mike. Leaving him so soon didn't sound good, but she really wanted his stalker caught, and if she was honest, she wanted to be at her restaurant.

"They already have, caught up with her before she left for church this morning," Gunner said. "Apparently, she claims she goes to your dad's church and would never harm your family." Gunner gave Mike a significant look.

Shar thought that was very interesting. So this Meredith had been at school with them at Auburn, but now she lived in Birmingham and had infiltrated her way into Mike's family?

"Of course, she denies that she would ever hurt you either. She even let the police search her computers and her condo. She invited them right in without a search warrant, and she has an alibi for last night. Apparently, she and the guy we saw her with had dinner then took a late flight back to Birmingham. She had proof of the flight. There's no way she started the dumpster fire."

Shar's eyes widened. Meredith inviting the police into her condo without a warrant definitely didn't sound like a guilty person.

"The police found nothing at her condo. The more disturbing thing is when the teenager at Hilton Head and the computer guys from the university saw a picture of Meredith, they all said the lady looked a lot like her, but it wasn't her."

Shar's too-full stomach tumbled. "So somebody's setting her up?"

"It looks that way." Gunner leaned back against his chair and blew out a breath. "I mean, she just fits too perfectly. She's known you since college, and you broke her heart and told her you left her for your career. Everything points to her, but my gut is saying it's a setup."

"So basically we've got ... nothing?" Mike held up his large hands, frustration in his face.

Gunner shrugged. His jaw was tight, and his dark eyes troubled.

"Why would someone want to set Meredith up?" Lily stood and started pacing by the table.

"To throw us off the trail of the real culprit," Gunner said.

Lily nodded. "Mike, can you think of anyone you've known since college, or before, who might have it out for you? Other women you dated and ditched, a man, or fellow teammate who might have been jealous of your success, or even some guy you stole a girl from. Anything?"

Mike pursed his lips, and they all waited as he thought. "I went out with other girls besides Meredith, and there were a few guys on the football team who might've felt I took their playing time."

"Okay, write them all down while we clean up breakfast." Lily stood and started stacking dishes. Shar helped her.

Gunner found Mike a piece of paper and a pen, and she heard Mike say, "It'd be a lot easier to just text it to you."

"Sorry, man, I shut down your phone."

Mike looked pretty frustrated, and Shar knew how he felt as Gunner had made her leave her phone at home. Also, the woman they thought was the stalker might be a dead end. She was a fan of more time with Mike, but not of sitting around doing nothing and waiting. How long were they going to be shut up in this cabin?

Mike searched his brain and came up with six different men and women who might possibly have a reason to come after him and threaten the women he dated like the stalker did, but they were all a stretch in his mind. One name kept coming to him, and he kept dismissing it, but then he finally wrote at the bottom, Brett White. He felt like such a jerk even naming his friend, but once he thought of it, he couldn't put it from his mind. Brett had always seemed so positive and cool, but there were times Mike had caught him giving him a look that was full of envy. Hopefully, he was just imagining it, because he really liked the guy, and Mike felt bad that he'd taken Brett's spot on the Patriots.

He handed the list off to Gunner, then asked him, "Shar and I would love to go on a hike. What do you think?"

Gunner nodded. "We can all go. Just let Lily and I get some weapons on."

"Okay. Shar and I will get our shoes on." Mike tried to inject a funny note in his voice. Who just puts weapons on? Gunner and Lily. Gunner gave him a very minuscule courtesy smile.

He turned to Shar as she walked out of the kitchen. "Gunner says we can go on a hike after he and Lily strap their weapons to their bodies."

Shar laughed. "I left all my weapons home. What should I bring?"

"Just your pretty face."

She blushed even prettier. Mike didn't love the situation they were in, but more time with Shar was not something he'd complain about. They'd lost the intimacy of last night when he'd been able to kiss her on her couch, but maybe over the next few days or weeks, they could regain it. Although, he really hoped they could find the stalker a lot faster than that. Somehow, he was going to play on Sunday. One week from today. He'd never missed a game, and he wasn't about to let some idiot stalker make him miss one this week.

Shar walked next to Mike's side along a trail through the beautiful forest. It was thick with aspens, poplars, and pine trees. The freshness of the air and yummy scent of pine reminded her of Mike's clean scent. It was all delicious.

Gunner was in front of them about twenty feet, and Lily was behind the group about thirty feet. Shar thought it was so interesting the way those two worked together. Interesting and impressive. They were obviously crazy about each other, but they put their work or assignment first. That had ticked Ally off when Gunner had put his suspicions before family. Shar thought any woman but Lily would probably have a hard time with their work, and the way it affected their relationship. Lily seemed to thrive on it.

"Do you think there are other cabins close by?" she asked Mike.

"I haven't seen any, but you'd think there would be. With power and water to this one, they probably did a whole development at the same time, but who knows? The trees are thick enough that it's hard to see too far."

She nodded. She liked doing something simple, like just walking next to him. "I wonder who broke this trail?"

"It's probably a deer trail or some other animal."

Shar liked deer, but what if it was another kind of animal? "What other kind of animal?" she asked, her eyes darting around the thick foliage but not seeing anything but trees and undergrowth.

"Maybe a bear or mountain lion."

Shar swallowed and instinctively stepped closer to Mike, bumping his arm with hers.

Mike glanced down at her with a concerned smile. "You okay?"

"I don't like bears."

"You're fine with alligators snapping at you, but a bear in the same forest is too much?"

"Yes! Alligators will usually leave you alone unless you dive in their pool, but bears will hunt you down and rip you apart."

Mike chuckled. "Don't worry. I don't think any animal or human is getting past those two." He pointed in front and then behind him.

Gunner looked over his shoulder at them and gave them a cocky smile. Lily really had softened him up. From the stories Preston told, Gunner wasn't the smiling type. Well, that answered the question if Gunner could hear their conversation.

Shar kept walking, realizing Mike was right. There wasn't much to be afraid of with Gunner and Lily, and all their weapons and training. Still, it was unnerving to be in the middle of a dense forest with bears, mountain lions, and maybe a vicious stalker tracking them. She leaned toward Mike again. He smiled and wrapped his arm around her waist as they walked. Shar liked the feel of his strong body close to hers.

She smiled up at him. "You're probably used to sprinting and working out hard every day, not just going on a mellow hike through the woods. Are you going to be okay?" Their hike was mostly level, and their pace was pretty slow, set by Gunner up front, who was scanning the area as they went.

"Yeah, I'm not used to taking any time but specific rest days off from training or playing. We'll have to set up a circuit back at the cabin. I can use the stairs for pullups, use you to bench press, and do box jumps on and off the landing."

"Whoa, whoa." Shar laughed. "Use *me* for bench press?"

Mike gave her a mischievous grin. "It'd be a light bench press, but I could do extra reps."

Shar pushed at him. "You don't even know what I weigh."

"One-twenty soaking wet."

Shar laughed. "You wish. I'm almost one-thirty."

"Ooh, that'll make the bench press quite a challenge." He rolled his eyes. Obviously, one-thirty was nothing compared to a tough NFL players' weight. She wondered how much he did weigh. Probably double her with all that height and muscle.

She smiled. She liked to tease with him. "We'll see how this bench press goes. I doubt you can even lift me five times."

"Oh! Don't insult me like that." His mouth twisted, and his eyes sparkled at her. "How about a bet? If I can press you more than twenty times, you have to ... kiss me. One minute of kissing for every rep I can do over twenty."

Shar pressed her lips together. That sounded like a win for her either way. "What do I win if you can't make it to twenty?"

Mike focused in on her with those deep brown eyes as they ambled along the path. "What do you want?"

You. She bit at her lip, unable to be that aggressive no matter how true it was. She'd wanted for him for a long, long time. She wished she could say a kiss, but that would be lame since he'd already said it. "Hmm. How about we snuggle on the couch on the landing outside our bedrooms, and I get to choose the movie we watch?"

"Sounds good." His voice dropped low and husky, and he bent down to her ear. "So it's a win either way because I bet I can talk you into a kiss while we're snuggling."

Shar stared up at his handsome face and almost kissed him right then and there. "We'll see how smooth of a talker you are."

Mike chuckled and pulled her in tighter to his side. "For you, I can be pretty smooth."

Shar sighed. Yes, he could. Crazily enough, the stalker and the fact that she'd deserted her restaurant didn't bother her much at all right now.

CHAPTER TEN

When they got back to the cabin, Gunner and Lily spent some time securing the cabin and the property, checking security cameras, and checking in with Sutton. But then they were both excited to set up a circuit workout for all of them to use and see how Mike did on his bench press challenge.

"Let's do the workout first," Gunner said after they moved furniture out of the way in the living area and set up the best workout they could without any weights. "Try to wear him out, so you win. What did you two bet anyway?"

Shar blushed, and Mike arched an eyebrow at her. "Who gets to choose the movie tonight," she said.

Gunner kind of smirked at her and said in a low voice to Lily, "I can think of much better bets than that."

She winked at him. "Yes, you can, lover."

Mike came up close to her, leaned in, and whispered, "I did come up with a better bet than that, and I'm going to win many, many minutes of kissing."

Shar inhaled the yummy scent of his fresh cologne and the promise in his voice that he was going to win. He was a professional athlete, of course he was competitive. She'd read an article on him once that shared his off-season workout, and she remembered something about how often he did bench press, but couldn't recall any specific numbers on how much he could press. She should've asked him for that number before she'd made this bet, but she was going to win either way, so it didn't worry her too much.

They had eight stations, so each of them took a spot, and Gunner started a timer and called, "Go."

Shar started with pushups then moved on to pullups, squat jumps, burpees, box jumps, jumping jacks, and v-ups. They did each exercise for one minute with twenty seconds of rest in between, which basically just meant getting to the next station. They went through five rounds, and she was barely moving by the end. It was an awesome workout for her, though she suspected it wasn't quite as hard for the other three, and she noticed how many burpees and pullups they were all able to crank out where she was lucky to keep moving at times.

When Gunner finally called, "Time," Shar leaned forward and put her hands on her knees, gasping for air. Sweat rolled down her back, and all she wanted was a drink of cold water.

"Nice!" Lily called out. She went around the room, slapping everybody's hands. When she got to Gunner, he grabbed her around the waist and pulled her in close. "No sweaty hugs," Lily protested, pushing at his chest, but she was giggling.

Gunner gave her a quick kiss, and Shar heard him murmur, "Your sweat smells like the dews from heaven to me."

"You crazy, crazy man."

"Only about you."

Shar loved watching the two of them together. Gunner was so tough and military, almost unapproachable, but he was soft and sweet with his wife.

Lily laughed and kissed him again, then she wriggled free and went to the fridge. She pulled out water bottles, tossing each of them a bottle.

"Thanks." Shar twisted off the lid and fully appreciated the cold liquid sliding down her throat. She got distracted watching Mike drink from the water bottle, the smooth muscle of his bicep flexing, and his beautiful lips around the small opening. Ooh, she loved those lips.

"It's time," Lily said, pushing her hip against Shar's, distracting her from ogling Mike.

The interruption didn't work as he turned to her, and all she could do was stare. He simply looked too good in a tank top and shorts. Of course, a professional athlete would be unreal fit, but to her, Mike's smooth brown skin and lean muscular body were irresistible. Add to that his sculpted, manly face, those sparkling deep brown eyes, and full lips that were so soft and appealing, and she was a goner.

Mike lifted his hand toward Shar. "Where do you want to do this?"

"The press Shar like a barbell?" she teased. Or the kiss? Her face filled with heat. She'd really like to shower before the kiss.

Mike chuckled. "Yes."

Gunner gestured to the plush rug in the living area. "You'll have to just do it on the floor."

Shar walked unsteadily to Mike and took his hand. She was a little awkward with Gunner and Lily watching but didn't know how to ask them not to watch. She and Mike walked over to the rug. He released her hand, laid down on his back with his knees bent, extended his hands up, and grinned at her. "Ready?"

"I'm not quite sure how to ... become your barbell."

Lily laughed. "Just lay on his hands, but keep your body stiff like a board, and he can press you up and down. Look, we'll show you."

Mike rolled up to a seated position as Shar stood awkwardly next to him. Gunner pumped his eyebrows, quickly laid on his back, and pulled Lily on top of him. She laughed as he clamped one hand around her hip and rear and the other under her armpit and chest. He pushed her up and down several times with her long, blonde hair streaming down into his face, a huge grin on his face, and his hands in positions that would be completely unacceptable for Mike and Shar.

"See?" Lily asked, beaming as she went up and down in her husband's arms.

"Um, that's not going to work," Shar said quietly.

"Why not?"

"Because we're not married," Shar protested.

"Oh! Sorry about that." Lily started laughing, and then Gunner started laughing. He lowered her onto his chest and released her, letting her fall on top of him. Flipping her over onto her back, he rolled halfway on top of her and kissed her long and slow. Mike looked away, and Shar wondered if he was anywhere close to as embarrassed as she was. Gunner finally released her, and Lily smiled up at Shar. "This is the most fun job we've had in a while."

"Oh, I'm glad." Shar supposed after tracking down drug lords and rescuing children from traffickers, this job would feel like a vacation to them. They were all safe in this cabin with the security she'd seen Gunner monitoring, and the stalker had no way of tracking them. Gunner and Lily were obviously letting their guard down. She didn't mind. If only she and Mike could kiss like that.

Gunner easily lifted Lily to her feet, springing up next to her. "Your turn."

Shar wondered if those two realized they had failed to show Mike how to hold her like a barbell while not touching her inappropriately. Her face flamed red.

Mike smiled up at her and extended a hand. "I promise I'll be careful where I hold you," he said as if reading her thoughts.

Shar appreciated his sensitivity, and she really wanted him to win lots of minutes of kissing, but she still didn't move.

"Please, Shar. I really want to win ..." His gaze flickered to Gunner and Lily, who were watching them with amused smiles. "My ... movie choice." His dark eyes warmed her clear through.

"I want you to win too," she murmured.

Mike's grin grew, and heat raced through her body. He laid down and bent his elbows so it wouldn't be quite so awkward for her to lay on his hands. "C'mere then."

Shar could hear Lily murmur, "Dang, these two are fun to watch," and Gunner chuckle.

She ignored them and focused on Mike. Walking closer on unsteady legs, she bent down close to him and carefully laid down across his chest, facing him. Their faces were very close, and his smile was big. His right hand gripped around her shoulder, and his left hand around her waist. He gently slid her to his right, along his body, keeping his right hand on her shoulder but bringing his other hand carefully down to her upper thigh, so he had a wider grip on her body.

Shar's stomach was so full of heat from him holding her and being so close to him. She was surprised at the way her stomach pitched when he quickly started pressing her up and down. She held her body as stiff and straight as she could, focusing on Mike's handsome face as Lily called out, "1 ... 2 ... 3 ..." Shar could hardly believe how fast he was going, but it seemed like no time at all before Lily yelled out, "20!" Then gave a cheer. "Yay, Mike!"

"Nice job," Gunner said.

Mike grinned at her, holding her with his elbows bent close to his chest for a second before murmuring, "You and I both know what I'm going for now."

"More minutes?" Shar asked, her body getting all warm again.

"Yes, ma'am." Mike winked, and then started pressing her up and down again. He didn't even seem to be breathing hard as Lily laughed and started counting again.

"... 34 ... 35 ... 36, Mike, how long are you going to keep going?"

"As long as Shar will let me." His grin was huge, and Shar decided she was absolutely in deep like with this man, but her stomach and head were protesting being lifted up and down like a barbell over and over again.

"I think you've won the bet," Shar managed.

He pulled her down close again and murmured so hopefully only she could hear, "But sixteen minutes is nowhere close to long enough. Can I kiss you as long as I want?"

Shar stared into his dark brown eyes. They could kiss all night long, and she wouldn't complain. "Yes, sir. As long as I get to shower off my stinky sweat first."

Mike released his barbell grip on her and wrapped his arms around her. "As long as I get to see you in just a towel after."

"Mike Kohler," she scolded. "Do you kiss your mama with that mouth?"

Mike laughed deep and throaty. "Yes, ma'am, and I'm going to kiss you with it too."

Shar was hot from head to toe, and she could hear Gunner and

Lily laughing behind them. She pushed off of Mike when all she wanted to do was kiss him here and now. Scrambling to her feet, she said quickly, "I'm going to shower, and then I'll make y'all lunch."

Mike jumped up to his feet and winked at her. "Sounds like a great plan, but when do I get my bet repaid?"

"Tonight, unless you tick me off before then," she shot at him, then turned and pumped up the stairs to her bedroom. She doubted very much he could do anything that would tick her off, and she could hardly stand the wait for darkness to fall. Gunner and Lily would hopefully want some privacy as well because all she wanted was time alone with that beautiful man.

CHAPTER ELEVEN

Shar was anxious and excited about all those minutes of kissing that Mike had earned as the day slowly progressed. She enjoyed being around Gunner, Lily, and most of all, Mike, but at the same time, she was wishing away each moment of daylight.

Lily and Gunner kept sharing secretive looks, and Mike kept giving Shar smoldering glances as they ate and made a fuss over Shar's vegetable soup and Waldorf salad for lunch. Then, they played card games and watched a movie to pass the time in the afternoon. Shar really enjoyed snuggling close to Mike during the movie, but she wanted more. She wanted to kiss him and never come up for air. While Gunner checked every-thing outside, monitored security, and spent more time on the phone discussing the people Mike had written down with Sutton, the rest of them worked together to make a seafood scampi, homemade breadsticks, and seared vegetables for dinner. Shar worried that Lily had eaten a similar pasta last night, but Lily reassured her she would be more than happy to eat it again.

Dinner turned out fabulous, and Shar was blushing from all the compliments, especially loving how much Mike seemed to enjoy it. They all talked and laughed together as they ate and cleaned up after. Gunner could actually be funny, but Shar still thought he'd married up. Lily was amazing. After they cleaned up dinner, they sat around in the living area, talking. Shar felt like she and Mike were just waiting for the moment it was acceptable to say they were going up to bed. Not that they were going to bed together, but that they would finally get those minutes of kissing she'd been daydreaming about all day.

"Any news from Sutton?" Mike asked.

Shar really liked that they all were part of this. Gunner didn't seem to be hiding anything from them. He and Lily were a great team, and Mike included her in the conversation.

Gunner straightened on the couch, and his dark eyes got more serious. "They haven't found any red flags about most of the names on your list."

Shar felt the swoop of disappointment. Would they ever find this stalker?

"But Sutton is concerned about Brett White."

Shar straightened and glanced at Mike. "The wide receiver for the Giants is on your list?"

He nodded tightly. "He called this morning, and I couldn't put the name from my mind as I wrote the list. I felt bad about it, though. He's been my friend since college, and actually I've known him since high school."

Since college? Shar could understand why Mike would feel bad about naming his fellow player and friend.

"There are a few red flags with Brett, besides the fact that the timing works, and he has the means to coordinate the stalking or hire somebody to," Gunner started explaining. "He's got reasons to hate you for winning the Male Athlete of the Year over him in college, taking his spot on the Patriots, and really, just being the all-star. But there's some other info that Sutton's guys uncovered, actually through one of Preston's old college buddies who plays for the Giants. I guess Brett was bragging that he was going to get your spot on the Patriots to somebody in the locker room before their early afternoon game. When Preston's friend overheard him and asked him about it, he clammed up, said he was just joking. Preston got a text about it and passed on the info to Colt."

"But that could just be a player bragging, and the jealousy thing is nothing new. These guys are highly competitive, and all want to be the best," Lily said.

Mike nodded. "Even if he was my stalker, what's the play? He's trying to upset me enough to make me not play well, so he takes my spot?"

Gunner shrugged. "A lot of players are head cases, right? Maybe he's hoping to make you one."

"Maybe." Mike shrugged. "So, nothing else?"

"Sutton is concerned enough that he's got two men trying to find Brett to question him."

"What do you mean trying to find him? He had the one o'clock start today. He should just be flying home with the team."

"Should be, but he's not on that plane."

The room went quiet. Brett not being on that plane felt ominous, and looking out the windows at the world darkening around them, made Shar suddenly uneasy.

Mike seemed to sense it. He slid his arm around her and said, "Don't worry. Gunner and Lily have us so safe in this cabin, an army could come after us, and they'd just laugh and take them all out."

Lily smiled. "That's right. You two are safe. Do you want to ..." She pumped her eyebrows. "Head upstairs?"

Shar gave her a look but secretly loved the suggestion.

"Yes, yes we do," Mike said, grinning. He stood and reached out his hand to Shar. She put her palm against his much larger one, trembles racing through her at his warm touch and the depth of meaning in his eyes. This handsome, incredible man was going to kiss her, for a long, long time. She felt her stomach take flight. She could hardly wait.

Standing, she murmured goodnight to Lily and Gunner who were watching them with amusement. She walked close to Mike's side as they ascended the wide staircase. The loft was dark except for some built-in nightlights and the light coming from below in the main room. Mike paused outside her door and smiled down at her.

She heard Gunner and Lily's voices trail away, and then the master bedroom door close. She knew Gunner was probably monitoring the command center in there with all the security camera feeds and monitors, but she hoped the couple could enjoy some alone time.

She loved that she was finally alone with Mike, and her stomach did a happy dance as he rested his hand on the door frame next to her, leaning close and effectively pinning her against the closed door.

She shouldn't have, but she couldn't help but quip, "So do you have a timer? I want to make sure you get your allotted minutes."

Mike smiled. "I'll just count in my head."

"Ah!" Shar protested. "You had better not be able to count while you kiss me. I can't even think straight when you kiss me."

Chuckling, Mike eased closer. His strong body brushed against hers, and a flame lit inside her. "Hmm, I guess things were a little fuzzy in my brain the last time we kissed. We'll see if you can distract me enough to stop my internal counting."

Shar slid her palms up his chest, and he let out a low groan. She smiled. "Why don't you just forget about the timer?"

He arched an eyebrow. "So I get your lips for as long as I want them?"

Shar bit at her lip to hide the smile. "Yes, sir."

"Why am I wasting any time then?"

"Why, indeed?"

He grinned, pinned her against the door, and lowered his head toward hers. Shar slid her hands up around his neck, arching up to meet him. Their mouths connected, and joy exploded within her. Mike kissed her thoroughly, holding nothing back. His lips were just as delectable as she remembered from last night, as she'd always dreamed they would be. She knew they could kiss the night away, and she wouldn't complain.

Mike released her from the kiss and swooped her off the ground. She clung to his neck. "What are you doing?"

He grinned down at her. "I figured if we were going to kiss as long as I wanted, I'd better get more comfortable, or I'm going to get a crick in my neck."

Even though she got hot all over at the thought of being "more comfortable", she realized she only knew Mike as the superstar. Just because his father was a pastor didn't mean he had boundaries. "Mike Kohler. You'd better think again if you think you're carrying me into one of those bedrooms."

His eyes widened, but then they filled with warmth. "Shar Heathrow. You'd better think again if you think I'd ever disrespect you like that." He turned and carried her toward the leather couch set on the loft.

Shar cuddled in against his chest as he settled onto the couch. "Sorry," she murmured. "I didn't know where your value set was."

"It's okay. You don't know me that well. I'm about to remedy that." He grinned, tilted her chin up with his palm, and proceeded to kiss away all her worries and rational thought. Shar loved every second of being held tightly against him as they kissed.

Suddenly, an alarm blared through the cabin. Shar jerked away from Mike, and her heart started racing fast for a completely different reason than his unreal kisses. Mike lifted her easily to her feet, stood, and took her hand. They hurried to the stairs and down them. Gunner burst out of the master suite with guns and knives strapped to his body like some kind of Rambo. Lily was right behind him. She had a pistol in hand.

"What's going on?" Mike asked.

"I've got three bodies outside according to the heat sensors, and that alarm is for fire. The system shows it on the back wall, but they somehow disabled the sprinklers. I'll dispose of the threat, and then stop the fire," Gunner said shortly. He turned and kissed his wife. "If something happens to me, you know the plan. Get them somewhere safe."

She nodded, her eyes filled with trepidation. "I love you."

"Love you too." He kissed her again before hurrying to the back door. "Arm this behind me." He slipped outside, and Lily quickly typed in the security codes to lock down the cabin again. She seemed to be taking all of this in stride, but Shar could see her hand was trembling. She tilted her head to them. "Get in the master. It's the safest spot."

Shar's body was shaking with fear. Three men out there, and Gunner was going to take them all on? And where was the fire again? Were they really safe in here? Mike wrapped a reassuring arm around her waist and escorted her into the master suite. "Don't worry," he said. "My money's on Gunner."

Shar knew how good Gunner was, but she could hardly believe he was going after those men alone. Lily closed the master bedroom door and locked it, easing to the monitors covering one wall. "I thought it was just another squirrel or deer, they've been setting off alarms all day. We heard a sensor trip while we were kissing," Lily muttered. "I'm sorry we let down our guard."

"This is not your fault," Mike assured her.

The bodies looked weird, like watching "Predator" and seeing the red that showed the heat from someone. Shar thought she knew which one Gunner was, but she counted the ones he was creeping toward, and it wasn't three. It was five.

"Lily!" she whispered harshly. "There are five of them. Can't we help him?"

Lily's face filled with indecision, her blue eyes looking tortured. Her husband, the man she loved, was outside fighting five men. How could she not go to him? Was her sense of duty for protecting Mike and Shar that strong? They heard a gunshot and a shout, and Shar screamed as she saw one weird red shape hit the ground, but the other four turned and flew toward Gunner.

Mike's jaw clamped tight. "I'm going to help him." He strode toward the door.

Lily jumped in front of him. "You're not trained. You'd just be a liability."

"I can fight," he said, lifting her off her feet and to his side. He strode toward the door, but Lily slid underneath him, knocking his feet out. Mike hit the floor on his knees.

Lily sprang onto his back, wrapping her arms tight around his neck as more gunshots rang outside. "You think I don't want to help him?" she ground out. "This is killing me."

Shar gasped. "Don't fight each other," she begged them, hurrying to help, but she didn't know who to help either. She didn't want Mike going out there, but she also didn't want Gunner dying. But then she smelled ... smoke.

"Fire!" Shar yelled. Smoke was oozing under the closed door.

Mike and Lily sprang apart. Lily went to the security station. "The kitchen wall's on fire," she said. "I have to get you two out of here." She glanced at the screens, and everything was a blur as the bodies were obviously engaged in deep combat. Tears raced down her face as she turned away and motioned. "Let's go. The Escalade is bulletproof. Sutton's guys are an hour out, but we can start their direction."

"But Gunner ..." Shar could not believe Lily could leave him behind.

Lily swallowed hard and said, "Will take them out. I have my assignment. Move!"

They followed her out of the master bedroom. Smoke poured from the mudroom behind the kitchen, and flames were licking the bottom of the kitchen cabinets.

"They'll expect us to come out the front door," Lily said.

"Like we have a choice?" Shar was trembling from head to toe. Gunner was going to be killed, and then these men were going to mow them down as they tried to escape.

Lily smiled despite the turmoil in her eyes. She went toward the roaring fire in the kitchen. Mike started after her. "Lily!"

She flipped a plush rug off the wood floor, revealing a trap door. Yanking it open, she gestured down. "Let's go."

She led the way down a steep staircase. Mike escorted Shar in front of him and took up the rear, closing the trapdoor behind him, probably to prevent the fire from rushing down it like a chimney chute. Being sealed in the dark made Shar feel claustrophobic and horrified. It smelled damp and moldy. Lily flicked on her cell phone light, and Shar cautiously followed the bobbing light. They finally reached the bottom of the staircase and went along a tunnel of sorts. Maybe a dozen feet later, Lily cautioned, "Stairs up."

Shar blindly felt her way, tripping on one stair. Mike's hand shot out and held her waist to help her. She appreciated his quiet support but couldn't stop shaking. Five men out there. Hired mercenaries? Mike's stalker had seemed like a deranged fan or bitter ex-girlfriend or rival, not someone who could track them to their safe house, set it on fire, disable the sprinkling system, divide their protection, and take out Gunner. No, she didn't know they'd taken out Gunner, but how could he win against five men?

"Stay here until I let you know it's safe." Lily shut off her cell phone light, pushed open another trap door, and climbed into the dimly lit detached garage where they'd parked the Escalade.

Shar paused on the steps. Mike put his hand on her waist, reassuring her that he was there. Mike was a well-built guy, and he claimed he could fight, but as Lily said, he wasn't trained. If these guys were mercenaries, they could easily best even a professional athlete like Mike. Especially if they simply shot him. Those gunshots she'd heard made her sick. What if they'd already shot Gunner and were now simply waiting for them to leave the safety of the house because of the fire?

From the other side of the trap door, she heard a grunt and a thump, and then the sounds of fists hitting flesh.

Mike pushed past her. "Stay here," he commanded.

Shar wanted to grab him and keep him from being hurt, but she also wanted him to help Lily if he could. There was obviously at least one bad guy waiting in the garage to prevent them from escaping. What if there was more than one? Shar definitely knew she couldn't just "stay here". She crept up the steps and could see out the windows that the back of the cabin was almost engulfed in flames, shooting up to the sky. Were they so remote that no neighbor would raise the alarm or come help? Yet she didn't want anyone else being hurt and knew they were a long way from a police or fire station.

She focused on the people highlighted in the dim garage. Lily was fighting some guy in black. Mike grabbed the guy from behind and wrenched his arms behind his back. "Get some rope," he said to Lily.

She nodded and turned, grabbing rope off the nearby workbench. Mike wrestled the guy to the ground, and Lily proceeded to hogtie him so fast, Shar couldn't help but be impressed.

"How many men?" Lily asked him.

"Too many for a little girl like you to take on," the guy grunted out.

Lily stood. "I took you on."

"You're all dead," the man grunted.

Lily ignored him and hurried toward the driver's side of the Escalade. "Get in."

Mike opened the back door for Shar. She scrambled in, and he shut it, climbing in the passenger seat. Lily pushed open the garage and drew in a tremulous breath, "Here goes."

Shar still couldn't believe she would leave her husband. She leaned up between the front seats. "Gunner?"

Lily bit at her lip and shook her head. "I have to protect you," she forced out.

Shar didn't ask anything else. How could Lily do a job like this where she could lose the love of her life at any moment? Shar knew it was a noble job to protect others, but she could not imagine such a life. If she could ever settle down with someone amazing like Mike, she would just hold him close and not risk losing him.

The door opened silently and quickly. Lily gunned it out of the garage. The cabin lit up the night with orange flames. Shar's eyes darted around for Gunner and the other men who fifteen minutes ago had been fighting by the cabin. She waited for gunshots to ping off the Escalade as they flew away from the garage, but besides the roar of the fire, all was eerily quiet.

"Where are they?" Mike asked.

"I don't know, but Sutton's men are coming. They'll help Gunner, and you'll be safe." Lily gripped the steering wheel tightly. Tears traced down her pretty face as she sped away from her husband, who might be dead even as they drove away.

"You said they're an hour out," Shar couldn't help but remind her.

Lily just gripped the steering wheel tighter, shaking her head and biting at her lip but still not stopping the tears that kept coming. Shar's heart was breaking for her. She was grateful that Lily was keeping them safe, but she couldn't stand the thought of leaving Gunner behind.

"We can't leave him," Mike declared.

"They're after you," Lily reminded him. "If we go, they'll follow us, and maybe ... He's the best fighter I've ever seen. He'll be okay." She brushed the wetness from her eyes as they flew down the tree-lined drive.

Across the road up ahead, a body lay in the dirt.

"Stop!" Mike yelled.

"Gunner!" Lily yelled louder, slamming on the brakes.

The Escalade jerked to a stop, and Lily flung open her door. "You stay inside," she demanded. "Weapons in the glove box."

Lily slammed her door shut and ran to her husband's body.

Shar couldn't hold back the sob or blink back the tears stinging her eyes as she watched Lily fling herself over Gunner's inert form, and heard her wail, "No!"

Mike yanked open the glove box and pulled out a gun and a knife.

Men filtered in from the trees toward Lily and Gunner. They

looked eerie and terrifying in all black with weapons trained on Lily.

"Mike," Shar whispered in horror. They'd driven right into an ambush.

He glanced back at her. "Stay in here. If we all get killed, you drive over us and get to safety."

Shar's eyes widened at the horrific picture he'd just painted. "No ... Mike!"

But he was already pushing the door open and jumping out to confront the men.

Shar stared as Lily jumped in front of Gunner's body to face the four men who were surrounding her. She looked defiant and brave, but these men had obviously taken out Gunner. There had been five heat signatures fighting Gunner earlier so they'd only lost one of their group in the battle. How could Lily win against them when Gunner had failed?

Mike roared from behind them. "You want me? Here I am!"

They all spun to face him. Dressed in black, three of the men looked like trained warriors. She only recognized the face of the man who looked like an athlete: Brett White.

There was no way Shar was staying huddled in this vehicle if she could be of any help. She'd never even been in a fight, but she could at least be a distraction if need be. She slid open the door, but unfortunately, the interior light turned on and highlighted her. She eased down to the dirt, quietly shutting the door behind her, but the men noticed her exit.

"Aw, the newest conquest, eh Mike? She's gorgeous. Can't wait to carve up that pretty face," Brett sneered.

Mike glanced back at her. "Shar, get back in the car."

She shook her head, resolutely. "I'll fight with you."

Brett chuckled. "Isn't that sweet? You always got the women's devotion, didn't you, Mike?"

Mike gestured her back, talking to distract Brett. "I can't believe you'd do this. I thought we were friends."

Brett smiled sinisterly. "I've always hated you. Mike Kohler: the chill, benevolent athlete who helps out the orphans and the homeless. When Meredith Ulysses wouldn't ditch you for me, and then you won the 'Male Athlete of the Year', and *then* you got the spot over me on the Patriots." His face became ugly and twisted. "I knew I'd do anything to mess you up. Threatening your dates and almost taking a few of them out was fun, and I hoped it was messing with your head, but when my agent found out I could have your spot on the Patriots if I took you out? I started really planning." He gestured around at Gunner lying there and Lily standing in front of him. The cabin on fire. Mike exposed.

"I got you scared enough to go into hiding and was able to trace your location when you answered my call. Your security guy was tough, four against one, and he would've taken out more than just one of my guys if Jake hadn't finally split his head open with a two by four." He smirked. "Now he's dead and I'm going to kill all of you, and no one will ever be able to trace it back to me. I think I'll start with Ally Steele's pretty twin sister. Make you watch me have my fun with her before I kill her, then kill you."

He tilted up his chin to Shar. "Hey, beautiful. You ready for a real man?"

"Never!" Shar flung at him.

"You won't touch her," Lily hollered. The men swung to face her. She leveled her handgun and shot one of the men in the head. He went down and didn't move. The two other mercenaries whipped out weapons. Lily got off another shot, hitting another man in the shoulder and then throwing something at them before dodging off into the trees. A small explosion came from whatever she'd thrown, but unfortunately, the men dodged away and didn't seem to get hurt.

"Go get her," Brett screamed. The men took off. Brett whirled, pointed his gun at Mike, and fired a shot.

"Mike!" Shar screamed in horror as the bullet ripped through his leg and he went down.

"Get in the car," Mike yelled at her, grasping his thigh with his right hand and shifting the gun to his left.

Brett started toward her with a sinister look on his face. He dodged around Mike, who pulled up his gun and fired, but missed. Brett kept coming at Shar.

"Shar!" Mike hollered. He fired again. Brett yelped in pain, and Shar viciously hoped he'd hit him somewhere vital.

She turned and ran for the car, grabbing on to the door handle and flinging it open. But Brett grasped her around the waist and ripped her away from the Escalade. He wrapped his arms tight around her, pinning her arms to her sides and taunting Mike.

"You only grazed my shoulder with that last shot, and now I've got a shield I don't think you want to hit."

Shar flung her head back, slamming it into his nose. Pain ripped through the back of her head, but she heard a satisfying crack and a yelp of pain from Brett. She could feel warm blood spurting into her hair and realized she must've bloodied, maybe broken his nose. Good. His grip on her softened, and she yanked her right arm forward then back, digging her elbow into his gut. His breath rushed out in a pop, and he cursed. She jabbed the heel of her shoe into the top of his foot, and pain radiated up her leg, but Brett hollered again, so she figured it was worth it.

Grabbing her by the hair, Brett flung her to the ground. Her head hit the ground hard, and she cried out. Brett towered over her, glowering down at her and then over at Mike who had pulled himself to his feet and was aiming the gun at Brett. Blood streamed down Mike's right thigh and spurted out of Brett's nose. The fire popped and crackled behind them, giving the entire forest a weird orange glow.

Shar could hear the sounds of fighting in the woods and prayed Lily was holding her own. Everything seemed to be in slow motion as Brett pointed his pistol back at Mike. He smiled mockingly as if he knew Mike didn't have it in him to kill him. She wanted to scream at him to just shoot, but Mike clung to the gun without pulling the trigger.

"I guess I'll have to kill you first, then take advantage of your girl," Brett calmly said as if he had all the time in the world. "Sorry, you won't be around to—"

A gun retorted in the night, and a bullet ripped through Brett's chest. Shar stared up at him as his eyes widened in shock before he slammed back onto the dirt road. She scuttled away from him. Mike limped toward her. He helped her up, and she stared at him.

"Did you …" she asked as she'd never seen him pull the trigger.

"No. I would've to protect you, but I didn't."

They both turned, and Gunner was glaring at Brett's body, a semi-automatic in his hand. Lying on his stomach, he was propped up on his elbows, blood running down his head.

"Gunner, you're alive," Shar gushed out.

"Where's Lily?" he demanded.

Mike pointed at the woods. "She ran. Two guys went after her."

"No." Gunner pushed himself to his feet, swaying unsteadily as he clutched the gun. Blood covered his forehead, and he had to swipe it out of his eyes. Shar could hardly believe he was alive, but what about Lily?

"You stay with Gunner," Mike instructed. "I'll go after Lily."

"Neither of you can even walk," she protested. "Give me the gun, and I'll go after Lily."

"Shar, no." Gunner shook his head and started stuttering toward the forest.

Mike shuffled toward him, dragging his right leg. Shar hurried after both of them. Men! Honestly. Sure, she'd never shot a gun before, but how hard could it be? Aim and shoot, right?

A small figure darted out of the forest and knocked Gunner off his feet. He slammed back onto the dirt road, and Shar hoped the hit alone wouldn't finish him off.

"Get down," Lily yelled, from where she'd landed on top of Gunner.

Bullets sprayed the air where Gunner had been. Mike tackled Shar, wrapping her up in his arms to cushion her fall, but it still hurt taking the brunt of both of their weights and having the breath knocked completely out of her.

A man darted out of the forest toward them, angling for a better shot. Gunner rolled out from under Lily, firing the semi-automatic several times. The man was thrown back against a tree, and lay, unmoving.

"How many more?" Gunner panted out.

"That's all. I took the other one out in the trees." She grabbed his bloody face between her palms and kissed him fiercely. "Oh, baby, you're alive!"

Gunner smiled and then lay back in the dirt and closed his eyes. "Not sure I want to be."

Lily knelt next to him and tenderly cradled his head, wiping at the blood with her shirt. "You'd better want to be, or I'll smack you around after you get patched up."

Gunner's low chuckle came to them, but then he pushed out a heavy grunt as Lily had ripped her shirt off and was using it as a compress on his head.

"Careful," Gunner muttered.

"I'll give you careful," Lily shot back. "Stay still."

"I could use something to distract me from the pain," Gunner said.

Lily giggled.

Mike sank to the ground and pulled Shar down with him. "Are you okay?" she asked anxiously.

"Just a flesh wound." He gave her a brave smile, but then he followed Lily's example, pulled off his shirt, and pressed it into the wound on his leg. His smile was a little more grim. "But I'm not sure how much more blood I want to lose before help gets here."

Shar wasn't even sure how to help him, or what to do. She wanted to hold him and kiss him, but he'd taken a bullet and had lost a lot of blood. He pressed the wound with his right hand, wincing slightly, and opened his left arm to her. "I could use you close," he said.

Shar smiled and cuddled into his side. He wrapped his arm around her waist and stared down at her. Softly kissing her forehead, he let out a shudder. "I can't put the memory of Brett threatening you out of my mind."

Shar put a finger over his glorious lips. "Shh. I'm okay. You were amazing."

Mike chuckled. "I don't know about amazing. Watch me play on Sunday, and then you'll think amazing. I'll let Gunner and Lily have the glory on this field."

Those two were suspiciously quiet. Shar hoped they were kissing and not both passed out.

Shar smiled at Mike. "I would love to cheer for you on Sunday, but Mike ..." She pointed to his leg. "I don't know that you'll be playing for a while."

He cursed softly.

"Do you kiss your mama with that mouth?" she asked.

Mike gave her a sheepish grin but shot right back. "Yes, and I'm going to kiss you with it too."

"Be my guest."

Mike bent his head toward hers and tenderly explored her mouth with his. The fire burned behind them, and if Gunner was still conscious, he and Lily were probably having their own kissing session across the way. Shar let herself concentrate on kissing the superstar of her dreams. She also let her fingers and palms explore the glorious contours of his bare chest and back.

Sirens and flashing lights disturbed their kiss, but she still didn't pull away. Soon enough, they'd have to face the aftermath of this mess and daylight. For now, she was going to kiss Mike until someone pulled them apart.

CHAPTER TWELVE

Shar's head lolled to the side as she waited in Mike's hospital room for him to wake up. It was early Monday morning, and he'd lost a lot more blood than the doctor had been comfortable with. Plus, the bullet had torn through his quadriceps and hamstring muscles.

When the EMTs had finally arrived at the cabin, they rushed Mike and Gunner both into the ambulance. Shar and Lily followed in a police car. The E.R. doc had put Mike out, giving him blood and operating on the torn muscles. Last she'd heard, Gunner had also lost a lot of blood from his head wound and had a concussion, but he was going to recover.

Too tired to hold her head up, she rested it against the bed railing and studied Mike's handsome face in the dimly-lit room. She loved his smooth, brown skin and full lips, but she'd love it even more when he opened those deep brown eyes and gave her a meaningful look. When would he wake up? She wanted him to rest and heal, but she also wanted to know he was all right.

Closing her gritty eyes, she said a prayer for him and a prayer of gratitude. They were safe. The memory of last night was insane and a bit fuzzy with no sleep and so much stress and terror, but somehow they'd all survived. Gunner and Lily had saved them from that crazy Brett White and his hired mercenaries. Shar was also grateful that Gunner had been the one to kill Brett. She didn't think Mike would've dealt well with killing his former friend. Mike was definitely a more sensitive soul than Gunner. She laughed to herself, thinking that was the understatement of the year.

She lowered the bed railing and rested her head against the tilted mattress and her hand on Mike's chest. His smooth skin was warm and felt so reassuring. She just wanted to be near him. It was crazy that she hadn't worried about her restaurant or anything but Mike last night or this morning. She hadn't known him long, but he was quickly becoming her entire world.

Sunlight peeked through the slanted blinds, and Shar jerked awake. Mike's eyes were open, and he was studying her. He still looked exhausted, but he was awake.

"Hey, beautiful," he murmured.

"Mike!" She gave him a gentle hug. "How are you feeling?"

"Drugged." He rolled his head from side to side then studied her. "How are you?"

"Tired, but so grateful we're okay."

He nodded. "Gunner and Lily were worth every penny."

She smiled. "True. Especially because they were your pennies."

He returned her smile, but his eyes were too somber for her liking. Studying her, he murmured, "I can't believe I endangered you like that. Please forgive me, Shar."

Shar pulled back. "It wasn't you. It was that crazy man, Brett White. You can't be blamed for that."

He shrugged slightly. "I blame myself."

"Well I don't, so stop being a dum-dum sucker."

Mike's full smile came then. He studied her for a few more seconds then his eyes drifted closed. "I hate how tired I am."

"It's okay. Rest. I'll be here." She could relate as she felt like she could sleep for days, and she hadn't had a traumatic bullet wound and a dangerous amount of blood loss.

He covered her hand with his as it rested on his bare chest. "Don't move."

"I wouldn't dare."

He smiled, but then his face relaxed, and she knew he'd drifted off again. His hand slowly slid off of hers and down to his side. Shar didn't mind not moving, staring at his handsome face and wondering what would happen between them when he got released from the hospital. He was going to need some time for his leg to heal from the gunshot wound. Hilton Head Island was a perfect spot for rest and recuperation. She smiled to herself and trailed her fingers across his strong chest, avoiding any tubes and sticky thingies on him.

Time ticked by, and whatever amount of sleep she'd had definitely wasn't enough as her eyes felt bleary and gritty, and she hoped she wasn't just romanticizing everything with Mike because she was so overwrought and emotional. But he had been so great, and she wanted to see what developed between them, now that the threat was over.

Her rear started hurting from sitting there, and she really needed to use the restroom. Mike was snoring loudly. It made her smile. She couldn't wait to tease him about it. Would he snore without all the drugs in his system and not sleeping on his back? She really wanted to find out, but they were nowhere close to a marriage proposal. They weren't even officially dating. She shoved away her fantasies of him begging her to date him and tried to focus on staying awake so she could be here for him when he awakened.

Finally, she could stand it no more, and she stood and stretched, rolling her neck around and then stretching her back and chest. Mike didn't stir. She hurried from his room and down the white, sterile hallway. Finding a women's restroom, she used it and washed her hands, peering at herself in the mirror. She examined herself through blurry eyes. Splashing some water on her face, she looked again, but nothing had changed. She still looked and felt horrible. The hospital staff had checked her out and cleared her, and then had given her some clean scrubs to put on. Her hair still smelled like smoke, though, and it was a rat's nest. Her eyes were puffy and swollen from stress and no sleep. Her lips were dry, and she missed the humidity of home.

Home. Hopefully, she and Mike would be able to fly there soon. She'd have to check in with Lily after Mike awakened and the doctor told her the plan for his release. She loved that she felt responsible for Mike. She'd heard his family had been informed last night about all the events involving Mike, but they weren't here yet, so she got to watch over him.

Exiting the bathroom, she took a long drink from the water fountain and then hurried back toward Mike's room. The elevator dinged open in front of her, and a bunch of beautiful people walked out: five women and one man. They were chattering, and only one of the younger women noticed her, giving her a friendly smile. With the scrubs on, Shar probably looked like a nurse.

Turning, they walked in front of Shar toward Mike's room. His family? They were all tall, dark, and beautiful like him, with the exception of one lady in the group who was a gorgeous blonde. So gorgeous, she should've been on magazine covers. The blonde and one of the young women walked arm in arm at the front of the group.

A nurse stopped them, and the man, a slightly balding older version of Mike, though not as thick or tall, said, "We're Mike Kohler's family."

"Oh, yes. I can definitely see the resemblance. Right this way. He's doing fabulous." The nurse led them into the room, chattering about Mike's injury and recovery.

Shar crept behind the group, suddenly feeling awkward and displaced. What was her role now? Did she introduce herself to his family as his ... girlfriend? No, she was only the crazy fangirl who he'd kissed several times, and who'd gone through something traumatic with him. They had no relationship, yet. Shar fought to keep her confidence up. Mike had shown every indication that he wanted to be with her. How to tell his family that? Hopefully, he'd wake up again and insist Shar stayed by his side, introduce her as ... she didn't know what, but she felt excitement and nervousness swell in her.

She stayed back from the room but could see through the open door and could hear their voices clearly.

"He's snoring," one of the younger girls giggled.

His mom stood on the left side of his bed with his dad right next to her. She brushed her fingers across his cheek. "Oh, my handsome boy. I hate what he's been through."

Mike's dad cuddled her close. "He's okay, love. He's okay."

She leaned against her husband's shoulder, tears trickling down her pretty face.

"Meredith," one of the girls said. "Wake him up for us."

"Okay." The blonde's voice was full of excitement, but Shar couldn't see her face.

Meredith? Could it be? His college girlfriend who had been framed as the stalker? Shar felt bad that the girl had been wrongly accused, but she still didn't want to leave Mike alone with the woman.

Shar started forward just as the blonde leaned down and kissed Mike full on the mouth. Shar gasped, but nobody in the room heard her. They were all tittering about Meredith kissing their brother or son.

Mike's arms came up around the woman, and it was obvious from this angle that he was kissing her back.

Shar's mouth and eyes widened, and her stomach plunged. No, no, no, no! She scrambled away, but not before she heard Mike murmur, "Now, that's a way to wake a man up."

His family's excited voices drowned out everything else as Shar spun and rushed for the elevator. She didn't know where she was going, but she knew she was going away from here. Hot tears stung her eyes as she pushed the elevator button and waited. A distinguished man who reminded her of James Bond, and a beautiful, refined blonde woman, walked out. She was barely able to squeak out a nod as she rushed in. They both whirled and came back in with her.

"Shar Heathrow?" the man asked.

"Yes?" she said cautiously, brushing the tears away and wishing she wasn't such a mess.

"Sutton Smith." He stuck his hand out, and she shook it. Then, he wrapped his arm around the woman. "My wife, Liz," he said with obvious pride in his voice.

Liz gave her hand a squeeze. "Are you okay, sweetheart?"

"I ..." She shook her head. The elevator went down to the first floor, and they all exited. She should've recognized the well-known couple. They'd been at Colt and Kim's wedding, but she hadn't officially met them. She was such a mess that she could barely see the entryway of the hospital in front of her. She was exhausted, emotional, and far too invested in what was happening with Mike and Meredith. The only answer that came was to get far away, so she didn't go start a catfight with some woman she didn't even know, and offend and upset Mike's family.

Sutton turned toward her. "What can we do for you?"

"Is Gunner okay?" she asked, wrapping her arms around herself to buy some time.

"Yes." Sutton nodded reassuringly. "Sadly, not his first or last hit to that hard head." He smiled. "Lily's giving him plenty of love and care."

Shar smiled. She really liked those two and was so glad they were both okay. She'd never forget watching Lily's heartache as she focused on rescuing Shar and Mike, and leaving her husband.

Mike. Shar's heart wrenched again. Maybe there was a logical reason he'd kissed that Meredith chick back, but Shar didn't think it was her spot to push in with his family and try to prove she was the one who should be waking him up. It hurt like a root canal throughout her entire body that he would kiss someone else and say it was the way to wake up. Shar was the way for him to wake up, not that blonde model.

"We were just on our way to see you and Mike," Liz said, in a smooth, beautiful English accent. "How's he faring?"

"His family is with him now," Shar managed to get out, but her voice bounced with emotion and probably betrayed her.

"That's brilliant."

Shar nodded tightly.

"And you're okay?" Liz's kind blue eyes swept over her face. She obviously knew Shar was a mess.

Shar was so exhausted and bleary that she could hardly see, let alone make any decisions. Some sappy part of her didn't want to leave Mike, but the small part of her that was rational quickly remembered he was upstairs kissing that blonde with his family surrounding him. "I just need to get back home, but I don't have my wallet or ID or anything to get on an airplane." Yes, that was the ticket, focus on getting back home, getting back to real life. The past few days with Mike were a crazy, unrealistic dream. She'd compartmentalize it and move on, back to her busy, fulfilling life running her restaurant. Mike Kohler was just a memory. A beautiful memory full of longing on her part, but it was done.

Sutton nodded. "We can get you home." He looked down at his wife. "You all right staying in Colorado for a day or so, love? I've got a few things to clean up with this case." He smiled wryly at Shar. "Someone burned one of my safe houses to the ground."

"Blimey, yes. Any chance I have to be close to you, I'll take it." She smiled sweetly up at him.

Sutton wrapped his arm around her and kissed her forehead. "Thanks, love." He focused back on Shar. "You wait right here, and I'll have a driver take you to my plane and fly you home to ... Hilton Head, correct?"

"Yes." Shar's lower lip trembled. They were so kind and so beautiful together. How would it be like to have a lasting kind of love like this? She'd probably never know. Her love and her life was her restaurant. That had been okay ... until she'd met Mike Kohler. "Thank you so much."

"It's my pleasure." Sutton pulled out his phone and murmured, "Excuse me for a moment." He walked away to make the arrangements, and Shar was left facing his beautiful wife. She had to be in her early fifties, but she still looked like a supermodel. Shar remembered when she was a duchess and named the most beautiful woman in the world.

Liz stepped closer to her and put a hand on her arm. "Are you sure you're okay, love?"

Shar nodded, trying to force a smile, but she could barely think straight. She must look a mess. Patting at her hair, she murmured, "Nothing a hot shower and my own clothes won't fix."

Liz's eyes were too perceptive. "Lily let slip that you might ... fancy Mike Kohler."

Fancy Mike? She more than fancied him. She thought she was falling in love with him. No, that wasn't right. She was a strong, independent woman, and he had his family and that blonde Meredith all over him.

"Are you sure you want to leave so fast?" Liz softly asked when Shar didn't reply.

"Yes," Shar said quickly. "I need to get home. My restaurant. My employees need me."

Sutton walked back toward them, pocketing his phone. "The driver is pulling up to the door now. We'll just wait with you so I can introduce you and make sure you're comfortable."

Tears stung her eyes again. These people were a class act. "Thank you," she managed to get out. "I'm so grateful I met you."

They both nodded graciously. Liz said nothing more about her "fancying" Mike, and Shar was grateful. The driver, a small, grinning man, hurried into the open waiting area of the hospital, shook her hand, bid Sutton and Liz goodbye, and waited for her to say her farewells.

"Thanks again," Shar said, shaking Sutton's firm hand.

He nodded. "Let us know if there's anything else you need."

"Thanks." She was saying it too much, but she meant it. These two had rescued her. She could've gotten ahold of Ally or Kim, and they would've helped her, but she would've been waiting a while.

Liz gave her another hug. "Wonderful to have met you."

"You too." She forced another smile, whispered, "Bye," and followed the driver out the sliding glass doors to a stretched Escalade limousine that she suspected was bulletproof. Sinking into the soft seat, she closed her eyes and let the tears leak out. Had Mike really kissed that Meredith back and said, "Now that's a way to wake a man up?" Oh, she could hardly stand to remember it. Even though it felt like she'd been hit by a sledgehammer, her brain still seemed able to remember.

She let her mind wander back farther. Mike using her as a bench press. Mike kissing her like she was the one for him. Mike grinning at her. A sigh escaped, and luckily, the driver let her have some privacy. She was going home, back to her restaurant. That had to be her focus. She just wished the tears would stop leaking out.

CHAPTER THIRTEEN

Mike was in a fog. He wanted to fight out of it and hold Shar close. She'd promised she'd stay close. He heard voices and movement and fought to rise out of the fog. Suddenly, lips pressed against his. Shar. He smiled against her mouth and wrapped his arms around her, kissing her through the haze. It was a subpar kiss for Shar, but she was probably as exhausted and out of it as he was. All that mattered right now was she was here.

When she pulled back, he heard people laughing, and he tried to joke away the lackluster kiss with, "Now that's a way to wake a man up." Their next kiss would be dynamite again. They were simply both worn out.

"Welcome back to the land of the living, son."

Mike finally opened his eyes. Everything was a bit blurry through the grogginess of the insanity of last night and the anesthesia, but his family was here. He could hardly wait for them to meet Shar. Where was she? She had to be close. Hadn't she just kissed him? His gaze swiveled around the well-loved faces until they landed on ... "Meredith?"

She grinned at him, biting at her lip. "Hi, Mike."

"Wh-what are you doing here?"

Her face flushed red, and his dad said, "Now son, that's no way to greet the woman you just kissed."

"I just ... kissed?" Horror traced through him. His head was cloudy for sure if he'd kissed Meredith and imagined she was Shar. Shar's kisses beat Meredith's a thousand times over. "Where's Shar?"

"Who's Shar?" his mom asked.

"She's my ..." Could he really claim she was his girlfriend? They'd only known each other a few days, but he felt as if they were together. And if it got Meredith to back off, he definitely thought it was worth claiming he was with Shar, even if he hadn't had a chance to clarify that with her. Where was she? "My girl-friend," he said firmly.

"Oh?" His mom looked confused, but then she smiled. "Well, then, we can't wait to meet her."

His sister Eliza glared at him. "Meredith came all this way to see you, you just kissed her, and now you're claiming to be dating some Shar chick?"

Mike had no clue why Meredith was even here. His father had taught him to be kind, but this was ridiculous. "Meredith and I broke up a long time ago," Mike said as kindly as he could. "Shar is the woman I want to be with."

Meredith's face crumpled, and she gave a little overwrought cry, spun, and ran from the room. Eliza gave him a death-glare and followed her friend.

As soon as they were gone, Mike turned to his dad. "Why on earth would you bring her with you?"

"Well, son, she's been coming to services every Sunday and for youth activities. She and Eliza have become close friends. She was with Liza last night when we got word about you being attacked by some stalker ..." He pushed a hand over his balding pate.

"And that means you'd fly her across the nation to see me in the hospital?"

"Mike, you're being a jerk," his youngest sister Kerri piped up. "Meredith's a sweetie. We all love her."

"Well, I'm sorry, but I don't. I haven't dated her in years, and I am never going to date her again. Can someone please find Shar?" Panic rose in him as he ached to have Shar close again. She'd said she wouldn't leave. Where was she?

Jacey gave a dramatic sigh. "I'll go try and find this Shar. What does she look like?"

"The most beautiful angel you can imagine."

"Oh, my goodness, it's getting deep," Jacey flung at him.

Mike chuckled. "Have you seen pictures of my teammate Preston Steele's wife, Ally?"

Jacey nodded. "I've seen her at your games."

"Shar's her twin sister."

"Okay." Jacey patted his leg. "Glad you're still in one piece, but I guess we're not going to talk about how you had a stalker for years and never told us." With that, she flitted from the room.

Mike looked at his parents' concerned faces. "I didn't want you to worry," he said lamely.

"All I care about is that you're safe," his mom said.

"Thanks, Mom." Leave it to her to forgive him instantly.

She bent down and hugged him, kissing his cheek. "A bath wouldn't be out of line, my love."

Oh, great. Had he driven Shar away because he was stinky? With the combination of smoke, hospital, and sweat, he probably smelled more disgusting than the locker room. No wonder she ran.

His parents had a lot of questions about the stalker, the attack, and Shar. Even though the despair of wanting Shar by his side was overwhelming, he felt himself drifting off again from the aftereffects of the anesthesia and losing so much blood. He jerked awake when Sutton and Liz Smith walked into the room.

"Cheers," Sutton greeted his parents. They all talked and chatted for a while. Mike fought to stay awake. He noticed Eliza and Meredith hadn't reappeared, but Jacey slunk back into the room sans Shar. What was going on?

Mike gestured her closer. "You didn't see her?"

"Dude, I staked out the entire hospital. I even saw one guy's gown flapping open, and got a glimpse of his nasty, and I might add hairy, rear." She pretended a shudder. "I did not see your Ally Steele look-alike. Sorry, bro."

"Thanks for trying," Mike said. He deflated into the pillows, semi-listening to the conversations going on around him. He didn't even have a cell phone to call her on, and her cell was still in South Carolina. Maybe she was so exhausted from no sleep last night that she'd found a bed to lay down on. She'd be coming back to him. She had to.

Liz Smith sidled up closer to him. "How are you feeling, Mike?"

"Okay." He looked into her blue, sincere gaze. Ten more seconds of conversation felt like running a marathon, especially without Shar here by his side. "Not really okay. There was a woman with me—"

"Shar Heathrow," she supplied.

"Yes. I thought she'd stay. Do you know?" He nodded. Even though he was bleary, he could see the light in her blue eyes. "You do know. Where is she?"

Liz gave him a compassionate smile. "She wanted to go home, so we sent her on our jet."

She *wanted* to go home? Without him? Worse, without even telling him goodbye and making plans for their future? He could hardly compute it. The Shar he knew and loved was feisty, strong, and independent, but she wouldn't just leave him, would she?

"I'm sorry, Mike."

Mike tried to drum up a smile, but everything was maddening and overwhelming him. Even listening to the conversations swirling around him made him want to shut down. Liz must've noticed, because she said, "Maybe we should take this party down to the cafeteria and let Mike rest for a bit."

Mike mouthed thank you to her, even though he was frustrated that she and Sutton would send Shar off on their jet. Yet, if that's what she wanted … His mom fussed over him some more, but eventually, they all filtered out. Mike thought he'd be happy to be alone, that maybe he could drift off to sleep and forget the nightmare of Shar disappearing. But, no matter how tired he was, sleep didn't come, and all he had were his thoughts. His thoughts were only saying one thing. He'd fallen in love with Shar Heathrow, and she'd ditched him.

CHAPTER FOURTEEN

M ike's leg healed a lot faster than his heart. The doctor said he couldn't practice or play for four to six weeks. He did as much of the workouts as he could and worked really hard at physical therapy, determined to make it four. Football was all he had right now, so he made getting back to full activity his life. Gunner and Lily got released and reassigned, and were heading to the south border of Mexico to fight trafficking. They said goodbye, but neither of them asked about Shar, which he found really odd and disturbing. He couldn't put her from his mind, but everyone else acted like there'd been nothing between them. Why?

He fought with himself almost daily, wanting to charter a quick flight out to Hilton Head and demand to know what happened, why she left when she said she'd stay. How she could be kissing and loving him one minute, then up and disappearing from his life the next. Yet, he didn't want to be the guy who couldn't hear no, who couldn't take a hint. He'd had many women pursue him, especially as an NFL player, who couldn't take a no. He hated the thought that Shar was telling him no by her distance and silence, but he tried to respect it.

The Patriots were playing the Titans on the Thursday evening game, and Mike was walking around on the field an hour before the game as other players were filtering in to warm up, and die-hard fans were finding their spots. But most of the stadium was still empty. On the far side of the field, he spotted the gorgeous face and dark curly hair that he would know anywhere. Without letting himself second-guess it, he stumbled through players until he reached her on the sidelines. Had she come for Preston and Ally? Who cared? She'd come.

"Shar," but the name died on his lips. It wasn't Shar. This person was rounder and not as tall.

Ally Steele flipped around and grinned. "Mike. How are you?" She gave him a brief hug. "Where have you been? Why haven't I heard your name dripping off my sister's lips?"

"I'd love to know that same thing," Mike said.

Other players were turning to look, but he didn't care. If Ally had any insight for him, he'd take it and praise her forever.

"Well, she won't talk to me about it. She claimed you didn't want to date her. She saw you with an old girlfriend, and that was it. Then, she shut down. Like a vault. She won't even come to the Patriots' games, and that's her favorite diversion on the planet."

Preston came jogging up, padded up and ready to play. He

hugged his tiny wife close, and Mike was jealous of their relationship and the fact that Preston was healthy and able to play.

"Hey, beautiful," he greeted her before focusing on Mike. "How's it going, Mike? When are you back?"

"We're hoping just a couple more weeks. Denver game."

"Awesome." Preston held out his fist to pound, and then went back to warming up.

Mike's mind was spinning. Old girlfriend? What old girlfriend? "Meredith," he suddenly said.

Ally turned to him. "What?"

"Did she see me with Meredith at the hospital? I still don't know why she presumed to come with my family and act like we were going to get back together."

"I don't know what you're talking about, but are you going to make this right with my sister or not?" Ally glared up at him with all the defiance and spice of a three-hundred-pound linebacker. Even though she was small, she was tough and had her massive, devoted husband to back up her sassy attitude. Mike thought she was great.

"I don't know. She just ditched me, Ally."

"Well, you listen here, Mike Kohler. My sister is the most amazing person on this planet, and if you aren't worthy of her, then you just stay here in Atlanta and whine about her ditching you. If you're half the man I think you are, get your butt to Hilton Head and work this out. You'll regret it for the rest of your life if you don't."

Mike didn't know how to answer her. She had no clue how many times he'd wanted to "get his butt to Hilton Head and work it out". But wasn't a relationship a two-way street? Why had Shar made no effort to contact him, to explain why she left? If she didn't want him, he wasn't going to push himself on her.

"Good to see you, Ally," he muttered and turned to go.

"Good to see you too, you lily-livered chicken," Ally shot at him.

Mike smiled, but he didn't stop. He didn't want to battle with Ally. He wanted to love Ally's twin sister, but it stung that she didn't seem to care about him at all.

CHAPTER FIFTEEN

Shar spent a miserable end of September and the first of October. She worked nonstop, which usually helped, but the restaurant wasn't as busy in the off-season. She didn't want to let any of her assistant chefs go, so she felt like she was just over their shoulders all the time. Ally constantly bugged her to come to Atlanta for a game, but she couldn't risk seeing Mike. If she saw him with Meredith again, she would have an implosion.

It was a gorgeous late Friday afternoon in October, with a light breeze but still a warm seventy-five on the island. She'd taken a break to walk on the beach as the lunch crowd was gone, and they were waiting for the dinner crowd to come.

Walking back up the path toward her restaurant, she eased onto the wooden planks and heard a voice from the side of her. "I need to speak to the owner. Alone."

Shar whirled, and there he was. Mike Kohler. He was still the superstar of her every dream, but it was even more encompassing now that she knew how amazing he was inside as well as out. She gasped and put a hand over her mouth. Some patrons arriving for an early dinner were gaping at him, probably wondering what was going on. Kelly rushed out of the kitchen and screamed, "Yes! He finally grew a brain and came. Yes!"

Mike smiled at the young girl but focused back on Shar. "I want to talk to you. Out back. In the alley."

Shar arched an eyebrow. "Sounds a little sketchy, Mr. Kohler." Her voice trembled, but she tried to act tough. "I don't have any knives on me, but you sure you're brave enough to go out there alone with me?"

Mike walked up to her, and she felt overwhelmed by his strong presence. "I'm willing to take the risk. Are you?"

She didn't know. Could she risk her heart to him again? After she'd gotten home that fateful day and slept for eighteen hours, she woke up and realized she'd been cruising along one level above zombie. And maybe, she shouldn't have run out. She'd replayed that scene in the hospital, over and over again. Meredith kissing him, and him returning it. Could there be another explanation? It didn't seem likely, especially when over a month had passed, and the jerk never came for her. He was the famous, amazing superstar, and she wasn't going to humble herself and chase him, especially after being accused of being his stalker once.

He tilted his head toward the rear of the restaurant.

"Go, Shar!" Kelly yelled.

Shar rolled her eyes, but she turned on her heel and strode off the wood flooring and around the back of the restaurant. She could hear Mike walking behind her, but she didn't so much as glance over her shoulder. Her heart was thumping wildly, and she wondered what he had to say. Would it change anything between them?

When she was in the alley, she rounded on him. "I'm here. What do you want to say?"

He towered over her, but even though she didn't know him as well as she'd planned on knowing him, she knew she was physically safe with him, but probably not emotionally.

"First of all," he started, "you promised you wouldn't leave my hospital room, and you did. Why?"

Her eyes narrowed. "I had to use the restroom. If you must know."

"Why didn't you come back?"

She swallowed down the awful memory and spit out, "I figured you didn't need me when you had Meredith kissing you, and giving you, how did you say it? 'What a man needed to wake up to?'"

"I was so out of it I'm not sure exactly what I said." His dark eyes were soft and regretful. He took a step closer. "Shar, I thought I was kissing you."

She took in a deep breath. "Well, that's all kinds of wrong. I'm sure I don't kiss at all like a fake blonde."

He smiled. "No, I'm sure you don't either, but I was pretty

groggy and out of it, and the last thing I remembered was you at my side, promising you wouldn't leave. Then I heard voices, and someone was kissing me. I remember thinking how the kiss was lacking but thought we were both just exhausted, and I wrongly assumed it was you. I'm so sorry."

Shar stared at him, trying to process what he was telling her. He hadn't meant to kiss Meredith. He probably thought Shar was the biggest jerk for leaving him.

Folding her arms across her chest, she bit at her lip and said, "I'm sorry too, Mike. I was like a zombie that day and so confused and upset. Seeing you kissing her and your family all there with her, obviously supporting her, I got ... really awkward and embarrassed. I made a horribly wrong assumption, and then, all I wanted was to get out of there."

"I can understand that."

They stood there staring at each other for a few beats, then she said, "So, what do we do now?"

Mike smiled and moved closer. Her back was against the wall. "Well, now I think we should most definitely pick up where we left off."

Shar's stomach swirled with heat. "I'm trying to remember where that was again."

He bent down closer. "We'd shared some unreal kisses, gone through a life-threatening experience, and you'd promised you wouldn't leave my side."

"Hmm." She placed her hands on his strong shoulders and sidled in closer. "Those are some pretty good memories, but I'm still at a loss for what we do now."

Mike bent down and softly, achingly, brushed his lips over hers. Shar arched up toward him, and he grinned. "I think we can figure it out."

Shar wrapped her arms around his neck and pulled him in tight. "Yeah, I think we can."

Then he swept her off her feet, his mouth coming down on hers. His kiss was full of longing and passion. Those beautiful lips she'd dreamt about took possession of hers, and she knew she'd been deluding herself the past month thinking she could be okay without Mike. This man captivated her, and for the first time in her life, she wouldn't mind putting a man before everything else, including her restaurant.

EPILOGUE

Shar glanced around the crowded suite, high above the Patriots' stadium. It was the day after Christmas, and the Patriots had just beaten the Giants. Her man had played brilliantly, and she loved hearing from the commentators how he didn't even show any signs of being injured earlier in the season. Mike and Preston had organized an after-party, holiday get-together in this suite for their families.

Shar stood with Ally, waiting for Preston and Mike to come up from the showers. All the famous and perfect-looking Steele family members were here, as well as Mike's distinguished-looking parents and beautiful sisters. Shar had gotten to know his family over the past couple of months, and they'd all been wonderful to her, even Eliza, the sister who was still friends with Mike's ex, Meredith. Kim and Colt, and even Shar's parents had joined the party. Everyone was talking, mingling, and filling plates with food from the generous buffet. Shar didn't mind eating food she hadn't cooked, but she definitely would've made a different sauce for the coconut shrimp.

Lottie Steele pranced up to them and giggled, "Twins. So *freaky*." She laughed and waved her hands at her forehead. Lottie was a gorgeous eighteen-year-old girl who had been born with Down Syndrome. She was extremely high functioning and even ran a charity with her renowned brothers and sisters-in-laws' help.

Gunner and Lily were close by, on a short break from saving the world. Gunner looked tough and unfazed by his injury. Lily looked beautiful and didn't leave his side.

"Can you tell them apart?" Lily asked.

Lottie pursed her lips and shook her head. "Nope. Both beautiful princesses."

Shar grinned and looped her arm through her sisters. "Ally's prettier than me," she said. "That's how you tell us apart."

"I don't think Mike would say so," Lottie sung out.

They all laughed.

A ruckus at the door announced Mike and Preston. The family all cheered and started hugging and talking excitedly about the game, Christmas, life, etc.

Shar could hardly wait to get to Mike, but a soft hand on her arm stopped her. She glanced down at Lottie. "What is it, cute girl?"

Lottie winked slyly at her. "Are you going to kiss Mike Kohler?"

Shar laughed. "Yes, I am."

"Can I watch?" Lottie's eyes widened with excitement.

"Sure, stay right by my side."

"Let's do it." Lottie giggled and waved her hands at her forehead again. Then, she grasped Shar's hand, and they started through the crowd. Mike spotted them and excused himself from talking to Slade and Mae Steele. Slade had an adorable, newborn girl in his arms, and Mae had a t-shirt on that said, "Mom life: #super-tired #superlate #superworthit."

Mike hurried their way, and Shar found herself tugging Lottie faster. Mike reached them, swept her off the ground, and then hugged her tightly against him. "Hey, beautiful."

"Where's the kiss?" Lottie demanded.

Mike looked down at their audience of one and grinned. "You want to watch a kiss?"

"Yeah, make it a doozy, Mike Kohler."

"I can do that." Mike bent and captured Shar's lips with his own. The kiss was all-encompassing and definitely a doozy. Shar heard the wedding march when it finished. She shook her head to clear it from her silly fantasies, but Pachelbel's Canon in D was still playing.

Mike smiled down at her and tenderly traced his hand along her jaw.

"Now, ask her," Lottie demanded.

Shar wondered what Lottie was saying, but Mike winked at her as if they had some secret plan. "What's with the song?" Shar asked.

Mike laughed. "That's Ally's doing."

Shar glanced around, and everyone was staring at them with expectant smiles. She focused back on Mike. "Does everyone know something I don't know?"

He nodded and dropped to one knee, clasping her hand in his. "Shar Heathrow. I love your laugh, your loyalty, your kisses, and your crazy sense of humor. Please make me the happiest man in the world, and marry me?"

"Like marry you this very moment?" Shar asked, still confused by the song and everyone staring at them.

"No, you dum-dum," Lottie sighed in exaggeration. "You've got to get the pretty dress first. Just kiss him right now, and say yes. Marry later."

Shar laughed, embarrassed. "I got it, thanks, Lottie."

She bent down low and kissed Mike long and slow. She heard a few whistles and catcalls, but ignored them. "Yes, I'll marry you," she said against his lips.

Mike slid the ring on her finger, stood quickly, and swung her around before setting her on her feet and kissing her with all the passion and love she'd come to expect from this amazing, dedicated man.

"Now, you're cooking," Lottie said from beside them.

Shar and Mike finally broke apart and started receiving congrat-
ulations from family and friends, Lottie first of all. Shar could
hardly wait to get the pretty dress and marry Mike. But this
moment, these people she loved, and most of all, Mike, were just
about perfect.

ABOUT THE AUTHOR

Cami is a part-time author, part-time exercise consultant, part-time housekeeper, full-time wife, and overtime mother of four adorable boys. Sleep and relaxation are fond memories. She's never been happier.

Sign up for Cami's newsletter to receive a free ebook copy of *The Resilient One: A Billionaire Bride Pact Romance* and information about new releases, discounts, and promotions here.

If you loved Shar and Mike's story, read on for excerpts of Preston and Ally and Gunner and Lily's stories.

www.camichecketts.com
cami@camichecketts.com

THE STRANDED PATRIOT

Ally strode toward Mike Kohler and Preston Steele, dodging around people in the crowded ballroom. She'd almost reached them when Preston glanced her direction and the world around her disappeared. Their gazes locked, and she was lost in the delicious indulgence of chocolate brown. His beautifully sculpted face had nothing on the power of his warm gaze. Never in her life had a man looked at her like that. Swaying on her heels, she prayed hard for inspiration. How to get him alone and beg him to help her, without falling prey to his charm or his handsome face. After Googling him constantly over the past few weeks, she'd learned that a man like Preston gave hundreds of women looks like that, women who were tall, thin models. At least he appeared interested and not repelled by her. That could work in her favor. For marketing, that was.

She tried to bat her eyelashes and give him what she hoped was a come-hither look, but she had no clue if she'd done it right.

She'd only seen those kinds of looks on television, never practiced them out on anyone.

Preston didn't break away from Mike and stride purposefully her direction. Not that she was surprised. She took a few stuttering steps his way, focusing on those deep brown eyes, and ran into someone's back. The contents of the guy's drink went flying, but luckily the liquid didn't hit anyone but the floor.

"For the sake of Pete," Ally muttered under her breath.

The man she'd smacked into turned around in surprise, but his face quickly transformed into a wide grin.

"Apologies," Ally said.

"No worries, but it seems I've lost my drink. Would you like to join me for a refill?"

"No, but thank you for being a chill cucumber about it."

He laughed. "Just one drink?"

"Maybe next time."

He held up his empty glass to her. She bowed slightly and turned away, focusing on Preston again. She could do this. She could do this. Confident woman, that was her. Confident in her hard work ethic, not her alluring smile. She was going to be sick.

Aiming what she hoped was a flirtatious smile at Preston and discreetly tilting her head toward the patio, she strutted away from the guy she'd hit and straight past Preston and Mike. She drew close enough to brush Preston's arm with hers, and she got distracted by his vanilla and sandalwood cologne. Oh, wow. Did all men smell that good? When she glanced over her shoulder, he was following her with his eyes. She tried to wink but failed as both eyes temporarily closed. Goodness' sakes that was awkward.

Easing out the side door, she was pretty sure the most desperate guy in Georgia wouldn't have gone for her weird little display. Hopefully the witnesses to her awkward flirting were few. Hopefully she could find Preston alone later tonight and march up to him without any stupid games, like she'd wanted to do all along. Why did she listen to Bucky? He was only her boss and she only loved her job.

The patio wasn't as crowded as the house, but there were still too many people for her to have the private conversation she wanted to have with Preston, if some miracle occurred and he followed her. Not knowing what else to do, she sauntered across the patio toward the flower gardens, hoping beyond hope that he'd follow her. She discreetly looked back, and her stomach hopped when she saw Preston's broad shoulders clear the doorframe. He was focused on her and moving fast her direction. Oh my goodness, it had actually worked. Yes! The makeover she'd paid for today must've been better than she thought. When she'd looked in the mirror, she'd simply seen the same rounded cheeks with a lot more makeup on, but it appeared Preston thought she was attractive enough to follow.

She debated stopping and waiting for him, but she wanted to make sure they were alone and out of earshot of anyone to have this conversation. There was also an undeniable thrill that she'd never experienced, being trailed by this powerful and handsome man. She reached the flower garden, and the heady scents of clematis, roses, and wisteria combined to make the moment feel even more mysterious and romantic.

Romantic? *Stop it, Ally*, she commanded herself. She wasn't here for romance; she was here for work, and it was guaranteed that Preston had no romantic intentions toward her. The way she'd felt when Preston met her gaze and then trailed her with his eyes was messing with her usually rational brain. She stopped underneath a canopy of trees and turned to face him.

Preston had a slight smile as he approached her. The way he filled out that tux made her stomach swirl with heat, and she clamped a hand to her abdomen. Had she ever been this close to a man this appealing? *Be calm, be professional.*

"Hello, Preston Steele," she said in a cool voice as if she had nothing riding on this conversation. Only her job, and the fabulous and charitable social media campaign that was her brainchild. Being attracted to Preston Steele could not factor in.

"Hello, Alyandra Heathrow."

"Ally," she automatically corrected. Arching an eyebrow, she found herself easing closer to him. "You know who I am?" That made more sense. He'd followed her because he was intrigued that the marketing person wanted to talk to him. Of course he didn't want to talk to her personally.

A slow grin grew on his face, making his cheek crinkle and robbing the oxygen from her lungs. Curse Preston Steele's appeal. She had never allowed herself to be affected by any man. How was Preston yanking her in so easily? The only thing that should matter to her was using his appeal to bring happiness to those going through rough times and in turn sell out the stadium, a harder feat this year with their newly inflated ticket prices.

"I know who you are." He also stepped closer, and his firm chest brushed her bare shoulder.

The suit coat buffered the impact, but Ally hadn't dated since middle school, and the contact thrilled her from her head to her painted toenails. She sucked in a breath and felt her heart thump faster.

"Head of marketing," Preston said. "The woman most of us try to avoid."

Ally blinked up at him. Avoid? Ouch. "What's that supposed to mean?"

"I'm not a rookie, Miss Heathrow. If you're giving me come-hither glances and brushing against me in a crowded ballroom, you're on a mission for Bucky. The question is, what do you and Bucky want from me?"

She'd let herself foolishly believe he'd followed her out here because he was drawn to her. *Stupid female feelings and fantasies. Focus on work.* "I need you ..." She paused and tried to think how to phrase it.

"*You* need me." His voice dropped, and its husky quality sent tremors through her body.

Their gazes got tangled up and she found herself being drawn closer to him, inch by inch. She could smell his delicious cologne, and the sheer power and draw of this man made her feel feminine and desirable and beautiful. It was all so unfamiliar and thrilling. Was he truly attracted to her? She knew he dated a plethora of rail-thin women. She wasn't his type, at all.

She didn't need him for her; she needed him for marketing. As her body eased toward his and she stared into his deep brown eyes, she couldn't have told you her mother's maiden name, let alone what her purpose was for miraculously leading this breath-taking man out into the gardens.

When they were inches apart and she was gasping for air at the meaningful look in his eyes, praying he'd reach out to her, he murmured, "You need me personally, or you need me because you're Bucky's lackey?"

That snapped her back to reality.

Keep Reading The Stranded Patriot here.

THE COMMITTED WARRIOR

Glancing around the quiet restaurant, Lily startled as she saw a man sitting in the corner booth. He was incredibly handsome with dark coloring, a well-trimmed beard, and a muscular frame, but he was also watching her intently. It wasn't a creepy look, more of a gaze of either interest in her, or possibly recognition. Aw, shoot. She hated when someone put together whose daughter she was, even worse when it was a man that good-looking, because she wouldn't let herself flirt with someone who knew who she was. No, strike that; she wouldn't flirt with anyone who wanted a claim to fame because they'd figured out her lineage.

It was the one luxury she allowed herself—flirting with handsome men. She rarely dated, as safety was her highest priority, and though she'd won every fight she'd been in, she never underestimated anyone or put herself in stupid positions; but flirting she liked, a lot. Tugging at her long braid, she hoped she looked presentable after rushing around a hot kitchen for hours. She'd given up on makeup, fancy haircuts, and manicures years ago, one more way to spite her mother, but she liked to be clean and presentable.

Lily gave him a forced smile that he barely returned. That worried her even more. If he was interested in dating her he'd smile or wink or something. This man appeared much too tough and serious. It was unsettling. She turned and hurried back into the kitchen.

Hanging up her apron, she called to the owners Kristen and James, "I'm out. See you tomorrow for lunch."

"Be safe," they both returned.

She smiled. They had no clue how many different places she'd lived over the past six years, some of them very un-safe, or the fact that she'd been trained by her bodybuilder of a nanny behind her mother's back and taken a variety of self-defense classes throughout the past six years. She was capable of protecting herself.

"I always am." She hurried back out into the restaurant before they could fuss about her anymore. The man in the corner booth caught her eye again. Sarah the waitress closing tonight should come wait on him, he'd be fine, but when their gazes caught she felt an unfamiliar connection to him. Maybe it was because he seemed to know her, but it might be something much more intriguing. His very build shouted safety and protection, unless he wasn't on your team, and his dark eyes tugged at her. She could see herself becoming a fan of this man.

Forcing herself to walk through the restaurant and past the deli counter, she exchanged goodbyes with the girls manning the counter and burst through the front door into the dry Idaho summer heat. It was after seven-thirty, but it stayed light until close to nine in late August. She'd be fine with daylight on the thirteen-mile ride to her lakeside home. Well, home was a loose word, but she loved her little camp trailer.

Walking around the side of the building, she found her commuter bike propped right where she'd left it and undid the lock. The lock was pretty superfluous in this little town, but habits were hard to break, and she didn't want to risk losing this bike. It was a good one and had taken her months to save up for, costing almost a thousand dollars.

As she pushed it toward the road, the front door of the deli opened, and the man from the corner booth strode out. The air suddenly became oppressively hot as she couldn't tear her eyes from him. The way he walked was like he was the world, so confident and appealing, yet not posturing or trying to put on airs. His very presence made her heart race. His dark gaze focused in on her, and he didn't play any games. He walked right up to her, stopped a foot away and said, "Hey."

Lily clung to her bike, so she didn't tip over. His sculpted muscles were semi-hidden by a soft t-shirt but nothing could fully disguise a build like that. His face was smooth and tanned with just enough facial hair to make her want to touch it and see if it was soft or rough. How would it feel if she simply brushed her cheek against it?

Instead of asking him if she could touch his cheek with her own, she sputtered out. "Are you just in charge of the *whole* world, military boy?" He was many maturity levels above a boy but teasing was imperative right now.

His eyes registered surprise, but he gave her a slight smile. "If I was, I'd ask you to dinner."

Lily's breath rushed out in a half-laugh, half-longing sigh. "Oh, you would, would you?" She flipped her long hair and pushed a hip out. "And where would you take me on said dinner, oh, hot and mighty one?"

His smile only grew slightly, but she could sense she amused him; he was simply a serious one. Ooh, he'd be fun to break.

He pointed back at the restaurant. "This place had fabulous reviews on Trip Advisor."

"Hmm. But I get food for free there so that's a pretty lame date."

His chin lifted, and his smile became a fraction more generous. She was going to have to work for a grin. Work, she could do. He was so tough and almost solemn, reinforcing her suspicions of a military background. He tilted his head across the street. "Should we try Big J's instead?" It was obvious from the sound of his voice he wasn't too impressed with what looked like an ordinary fast-food restaurant.

"Oh, I think I've got your number. You've traveled the world and think a simple fast-food dive is below you?" She arched an eyebrow and dared him to challenge her. He simply lifted a shoulder. "You'll have to be schooled then. It is completely unacceptable to use that tone of voice with Big J's. Their bacon cheeseburger could make you sing, and they have a pizza bomb that I'm salivating about just saying the words." He was making her salivate, but she didn't want to let on. What was a man like this doing showing up in her small town? She didn't know everybody in the valley, but she would bet all twenty-seven of the hundred-dollar bills she'd worked so hard to stash in her trailer that he wasn't a local.

"Salivate?" His gaze traveled over her face and truly made her salivate for more. "I'll have to try both of them then. You in?"

She was incredibly tempted, but it was a long bike ride in the late summer heat, and she didn't prefer doing it in the dark. There was no way she'd let this man take her home, and she hated to put James out as he lived the other direction of where she needed to go, up a beautiful canyon called Cub River.

"Not tonight, but thanks for the offer." She smiled and pushed her bike away, hating to walk away from such appeal.

"Are you working tomorrow?" he said to her back.

She glanced over her shoulder. "I've got the lunch shift." Yes! He wanted to see her again.

"When do you get off?"

She wanted him to smile fully. He was much too serious, no matter how much she teased. Still she saw no harm in getting to know him a little bit, maybe a date or two, maybe a kiss or two. His lips were a firm, manly line that she wouldn't mind a taste of.

"Four," she admitted.

"I'll be waiting for you right here. Then I can salivate ..." He actually gave her a larger smile. "Over the pizza bomb."

"What if I'm not ready to *salivate?*" she asked, winking sassily at him.

He shrugged. "Then I'll be waiting the next day, and the next day ... until you decide you are ready."

"Persistent, aren't you?"

He actually chuckled and grinned. The combination robbed the oxygen from her body. "Handsome" didn't do justice to this man when he grinned.

"You have no idea," he said.

"I guess we'll see if tomorrow's your lucky day."

He sobered and stared deeply into her eyes. "I guess we will."

The moment seemed to draw out between them, and Lily was lost in the depths of his dark gaze. This man had seen the world and the pain that was in it. Lily wanted to hold his hand and help him to see the happiness that was in it too. She hadn't known that happiness until she escaped her mother's clutches and found real people and the good Lord. Could she help him?

Keep Reading *The Committed Warrior* here.

ALSO BY CAMI CHECKETTS

Steele Family Romance

Her Dream Date Boss

The Stranded Patriot

The Committed Warrior

Extreme Devotion

Jepson Brothers Romance

How to Design Love

How to Switch a Groom

How to Lose a Fiance

Billionaire Boss Romance

Her Dream Date Boss

Her Prince Charming Boss

Georgia Patriots Romance

The Loyal Patriot

The Gentle Patriot

The Stranded Patriot

Quinn Family Romance

The Devoted Groom

The Conflicted Warrior

The Gentle Patriot

The Tough Warrior

Her Too-Perfect Boss

Fighting for Love: Return to Snow Valley

Other Books by Cami

Seeking Mr. Debonair: Jane Austen Pact

Seeking Mr. Dependable: Jane Austen Pact

Saving Sycamore Bay

Oh, Come On, Be Faithful

Protect This

Blog This

Redeem This

The Broken Path

Dead Running

Dying to Run

Fourth of July

Love & Loss

Love & Lies

Cami's Collections

Steele Family Collection

Hawk Brothers Collection

Quinn Family Collection

Cami's Military Collection

Billionaire Beach Romance Collection

Billionaire Bride Pact Collection

Billionaire Romance Sampler

Echo Ridge Romance Collection

Texas Titans Romance Collection

Made in the
USA
Lexington, KY